W9-BST-850

# PROMISE FOREVER

## MARTA PERRY

Indian River Area Library
3546 S. Straits Hwy.
P.O. Box 160
Indian River, MI 49749

Love Inspired.

Published by Steeple Hill Books™

If you purchased this book without a cover you should be aware that this book is stolen property. It was reported as "unsold and destroyed" to the publisher, and neither the author nor the publisher has received any payment for this "stripped book."

STEEPLE HILL BOOKS

Steeple
Hill™

ISBN 0-373-87216-X

PROMISE FOREVER

Copyright © 2003 by Martha Johnson

All rights reserved. Except for use in any review, the reproduction or utilization of this work in whole or in part in any form by any electronic, mechanical or other means, now known or hereafter invented, including xerography, photocopying and recording, or in any information storage or retrieval system, is forbidden without the written permission of the editorial office, Steeple Hill Books, 233 Broadway, New York, NY 10279 U.S.A.

All characters in this book have no existence outside the imagination of the author and have no relation whatsoever to anyone bearing the same name or names. They are not even distantly inspired by any individual known or unknown to the author, and all incidents are pure invention.

This edition published by arrangement with Steeple Hill Books.

® and TM are trademarks of Steeple Hill Books, used under license. Trademarks indicated with ® are registered in the United States Patent and Trademark Office, the Canadian Trade Marks Office and in other countries.

Visit us at www.steeplehill.com

**Printed in U.S.A.**

Indian River Area Library
3546 S. Straits Hwy.
P.O. Box 160
Indian River, MI 49749

# "May I help you?" Miranda asked, shoving through the inn's swinging door.

The tall stranger turned slowly. Afternoon sunlight coming through the front screen door lit broad shoulders, dark hair and an expensive suit that was far too formal for the island. Then he faced her, and her heart stopped entirely.

Tyler Winchester, the man she'd never expected to see again. The man who'd broken her eighteen-year-old heart when their marriage had dissolved.

The man who'd never known he'd fathered a son.

"Hello, Miranda. It's been a long time."

His voice was deeper than she remembered. More confident.

"Tyler." Pain ripped through the numbness of shock when she said his name. She hadn't said it aloud in years. How could two syllables have such power?

INDIAN RIVER AREA LIBRARY
3 8610 00033 601 0

Indian River Area Library
3946 S. Straits Hwy.
P.O. Box 160
Indian River, MI 49749

## Books by Marta Perry

Love Inspired

*A Father's Promise* #41
*Since You've Been Gone* #75
*Desperately Seeking Daddy* #91
*The Doctor Next Door* #104
*Father Most Blessed* #128
*A Father's Place* #153
*Hunter's Bride* #172
*A Mother's Wish* #185
*A Time To Forgive* #193
*Promise Forever* #209

*Hometown Heroes

## *MARTA PERRY*

wanted to be a writer from the moment she encountered Nancy Drew, at about age eight. She didn't see publication of her stories until many years later, when she began writing children's fiction for Sunday school papers while she was a church educational director. Although now retired from that position in order to write full-time, she continues playing an active part in her church and loves teaching a class of junior high Sunday school students.

Marta lives in rural Pennsylvania but winters on Hilton Head Island, South Carolina. She and her husband have three grown children and three grandchildren, and that area is the inspiration for the Caldwell clan stories. She loves hearing from readers and will be glad to send a signed bookplate on request. She can be reached c/o Steeple Hill Books, 233 Broadway, New York, NY 10279, or visit her on the Web at www.martaperry.com.

Therefore, as God's chosen people, holy and dearly loved, clothe yourselves with compassion, kindness, humility, gentleness and patience.
—*Colossians* 3:12

This story is dedicated to my wonderful editor,
Ann Leslie Tuttle, with gratitude.
And, as always, to Brian.

# Chapter One

Tyler Winchester ripped open the pale blue envelope that had arrived in the morning mail. A photograph fluttered onto the polished mahogany desktop. No letter, just a photograph of a young boy, standing in the shade of a sprawling live oak.

He flipped it over. Two words had been scrawled on the back—two words that made his world shudder.

*Your son.*

For a moment he couldn't react at all. He shot a glance toward the office doorway, where his younger brother was trying to talk his way past Tyler's assistant. Turning his back on them, Tyler studied the envelope. Caldwell Cove. The envelope was postmarked Caldwell Cove, South Carolina.

Something deep inside him began to crack painfully open. The child's face in the picture was partly shadowed by the tree, but that didn't really matter. He saw the resemblance anyway—the heart-shaped face, the pointed chin. Miranda.

The boy was Miranda's child, certainly. But his? How could that be? He'd have known. She'd have told him, wouldn't she?

The voices behind him faded into the dull murmur of ocean waves. A seabird called, and a slim figure came toward him from the water, green eyes laughing, bronze hair rippling over her shoulders.

His jaw clenched. No. He'd closed off that part of himself a long time ago, sealing it securely. He wouldn't let it break open.

The truth was, he didn't know what Miranda might do. It had been—what, eight years? He stared at the photo. The boy could be the right age.

He spun around, the movement startling both his brother and his assistant into silence. Josh took advantage of the moment to move past Henry Carmichael's bulk. He looked from Tyler's face to the photo in his hand, gaze curious. "Is something wrong?"

"Nothing." Nothing that he wanted to confide in Josh, in any event. He slid the photograph into his pocket.

"In that case…"

"Not now." He suspected he already knew what Josh wanted to talk about. Money. It was always money with Josh, just as it was with their mother and with the array of step and half siblings and relatives she'd brought into his life. The whole family saw Tyler as an inexhaustible account to fund their expensive tastes.

*You can't count on anyone but yourself.* His father's harsh voice echoed in his mind. *They all want something.*

"But Tyler," Josh began.

He shook his head, then looked at Henry. He could at least trust Henry to do what he was told without asking questions that Tyler had no intention of answering. "Have the jet ready for me in two hours. I'm flying to Savannah."

"Savannah?" Josh's voice suggested it might as well be the moon. "What about the Warren situation? I thought you were too involved in that contract negotiation to think about anything else."

He spared a thought for the multimillion-dollar deal he'd been chasing for months. "I'll be a phone call or a fax away. Henry will keep me posted on anything I need to know."

"Whatever you say." Henry's broad face was impassive as always. Henry was as unemotional as Tyler, which was probably why they worked so well together.

Tyler crossed the room quickly, pausing to pull his camel-hair coat from the mahogany coatrack. It had been a raw, chilly March day in Baltimore, although Caldwell Cove would be something else.

Again the image shimmered in his mind like a mirage. Surf. Sand. A laughing, sun-kissed face. His wife.

They all want something. What did Miranda want?

He shoved the thought away and strode to the door. He'd deal with this, just as he dealt with any project that went wrong. Then he'd bury the memory of his first love so deeply that it would never intrude again.

The bell on the registration desk jingled impatiently. Miranda Caldwell dusted flour from her hands as she hurried from the inn's kitchen toward the front hallway. The Dolphin Inn wasn't expecting any new guests today, and the rest of the family had taken advantage of that fact to scatter in various directions.

She'd thought she'd have an uninterrupted half-hour to bake some molasses cookies before Sammy got home from school. It looked as if she'd been wrong.

She shoved through the swinging door to the wide hallway that housed the inn's registration desk, along with whatever clutter of fishing poles and baseball bats her brothers had left on the wide-planked floor.

"May I help you?"

The tall stranger turned slowly. Afternoon sunlight through the front screen door lit broad shoulders, dark hair, an expensive suit that was far too formal for the island. Then he faced her, and her heart stopped entirely.

Tyler Winchester, the man she'd never expected to see again. The man who'd broken her eighteen-year-old heart when their marriage dissolved. The man who'd never known he'd fathered a son.

"Hello, Miranda. It's been a long time."

His voice was deeper than she remembered. More confident. Through a haze of dismay came the knowledge that Tyler didn't sound surprised. He'd known he was going to find her here.

"Tyler." Pain ripped through the numbness of shock when she said his name. She hadn't said it aloud in years. How could two syllables have such power to hurt?

He lifted his brows, eyes the color of rich chocolate expressing nothing at all. "Aren't you going to say you're surprised to see me?"

"I...yes, of course I'm surprised."

Tyler made no move to close the gap between them, thank goodness. If he attempted to shake hands with her, she'd probably turn to stone.

"What brings you to the island?" She managed to get the words out.

He seemed to move farther away from her, even though he didn't actually move at all. Maybe it was just the effect of the chill in his strong-boned face.

"Not a pleasure trip," he said crisply.

No, it wouldn't be that. Tyler probably vacationed in the south of France. He certainly wouldn't choose to come to Caldwell Cove after what had happened between them.

Maybe that didn't matter to him. After all, he'd had eight years to forget his youthful indiscretion. While she'd been looking at a reminder every day in Sammy—

Sammy. She sent a frantic, fearful glance at the clock. Her son would be walking in the door from school any minute now. As soon as he heard the name, he'd know who Tyler was.

But Tyler didn't know Sammy existed, and she had to keep it that way.

*Oh, Lord, please.* She sent up a fervent, desperate prayer. *Help me get rid of him before Sammy gets home.*

"You're here on business, then." She tried to sound as cool as he did, as if it were an everyday occurrence for the man who'd been her husband for one short month to walk back into her life. She moved behind the desk, putting an expanse of scarred oak between them. It wasn't enough of a barrier, but it was all she had.

"You might say that." Tyler leaned on the desk, the movement bringing him close enough that she caught the expensive aroma of his aftershave. "Maybe you'd better give me a room. I'll be here at least for one night."

Panic surged through her like a riptide. He couldn't stay here. "No. I mean, I'm sorry." She put both hands on the register to hide the pages. "We're all booked up."

His brows lifted again. "This early in the season? Try again, Miranda. I don't buy it."

When had Tyler become so sarcastic? That hadn't been part of the boy she'd married.

Her heart ripped a little. She didn't know him any longer. The boy who'd held her in his arms and promised to love her forever had turned into a man she didn't understand at all.

He was rich, of course. Winchesters had always been rich and successful. They were filled with the arrogance that came with always getting everything they wanted just by lifting a hand.

Once what Tyler wanted was her—shy little Miranda Caldwell, an island girl who hadn't had the least notion of the world he lived in. But that wanting hadn't lasted long. Just long enough to make the baby he'd never known about.

She swallowed hard, trying to come up with the words that would make him go away.

"I'm sorry, Tyler." She forced herself to meet his gaze. "I'm afraid we don't have room for you. I think you should leave now."

Some emotion she couldn't identify chased across his face, and the skin around his eyes seemed to tighten. "Leave? After you've gone to so much trouble to get me here? That doesn't make any sense."

"Get you here?" That was the last thing she'd ever do. "What on earth are you talking about?"

Tyler planted both fists on the desk, leaning so close their faces were scant inches apart. She felt the heat radiating from him—no, it was anger, so hot it threatened to singe her skin. His lips were a hard, bitter line.

"I'm talking about the little surprise package you sent me. Didn't you think I'd come down here as soon as I received it?"

She stared at him, baffled. "I didn't send you a package."

With a swift movement he took something from his pocket and tossed it to the desk between them. It fluttered onto the faded red blotter. She forced frozen fingers to pick it up.

Sammy. Her stomach twisted, making her feel as she had during those months of morning sickness. Tyler had a picture of Sammy.

No. He couldn't. Her mind moved slowly, struggling against the unthinkable reality.

With a quick, angry movement he turned it over in her hand. "Don't forget the inscription."

*Your son.*

The printed words struck her in the heart. They rang in her ears, mocking her. All these years of protecting her secret from him, only to have it blown apart by two simple words.

"Where did you get this?"

"You sent it to me."

"No!" The word nearly leaped from her mouth. "I didn't."

He made a quick, chopping motion with one hand, as if cutting her away from him. "Who else? I have to warn you, Miranda. If you want child support, you'd better be prepared to prove that boy is mine."

It took a moment for his words to penetrate, another for her brain to actually make sense of them. Then anger shot up, hot and bracing. How dare he imply she'd had someone else's child?

Common sense intervened. They hadn't seen each other in years. For all Tyler knew, she might have remarried, might have…

*He doesn't know for sure Sammy is his.*

Beneath the anger, beneath the pain, relief flowered. If Tyler wasn't sure Sammy was his son, she might still avert disaster. She wouldn't have to fear the nightmare of Tyler snatching Sammy away from her.

She stood up straight, trying to find the strength Gran always insisted was bred into generations of Caldwell women. "My son has nothing to do with you." She picked her words carefully. "I think it best if you leave now."

Furrows dug between his brows, and his angry gaze

seemed to grasp her with the power that had swept her eighteen-year-old self along with whatever Tyler wanted. ''I'll leave as soon as I'm satisfied, Miranda. I want to know why you sent this to me.''

His words rattled around her brain. Who had sent it? None of this made any sense at all. She tried not to glance at the implacable round face of the clock, warning her Sammy could walk in on them.

Nothing else matters. Just get him out of here before Sammy comes in.

''I don't know who sent it. I didn't. I don't want anything from you.'' It took a fierce effort to look at him as coolly as if he were a stranger.

He is a stranger, a tiny voice sobbed in her ear. He's not the man you loved.

Tyler straightened, his shoulders stiff, his face a mask. ''In that case, I'll—''

The creak of the screen door cut off the sentence, and fear obliterated her momentary relief.

''Hey, Momma, I'm home.'' Sammy's quick footsteps slowed when he saw that his mother wasn't alone. He glanced curiously at Tyler, then tossed a green spelling book on the desk. ''Can I get a snack?''

''May I,'' she corrected automatically. Cool, careful. She could still get out of this in one piece. As long as Sammy didn't hear Tyler's name, she was all right. ''Go on into the kitchen. I have some cookies started.''

Sammy nodded, turned. She held her breath. Almost out of danger. There'd be time enough later to sort it all out. Get Sammy out, and…

"Just a minute." Tyler's voice had roughened. It carried a raw note of command.

She forced herself to move around the desk, grasp Sammy's shoulders, look at Tyler. The expression on his face chilled her to the bone.

He knew. He'd taken one look at Sammy, and her son's beautiful eyes, so like his father's, had given them away. Tyler knew Sammy was his son.

Tyler couldn't stop staring. At first he'd seen a child with Miranda's heart-shaped face, her pointed chin.

Then the boy looked at him, and Tyler had seen the child's eyes. Deep brown, with the slightest gold flecks in them when the light hit as it did in that moment, slanting through the wavy panes of the hall window. Eyes deeply fringed with curling lashes.

Winchester eyes—they were the same eyes he saw every time he looked at his brother and every morning in the mirror.

Stop, take a breath, think about this.

He didn't really need to think about it. Maybe the truth had been there all along, beneath his initial assumption that he couldn't have a child. He'd known, at some level, that if Miranda had a son, that boy was his.

She hadn't told him. Anger roared through his thoughts like a jet. Miranda had borne his child, and she hadn't told him.

The three of them stood, frozen in place, the old house quiet around them. From somewhere outside came the raucous squawk of a seagull, seeming to punctuate his anger. She hadn't told him.

He shifted his gaze to Miranda, furious words forming on his tongue. He'd tell her just what he thought—

He couldn't. Not with the boy standing there, looking at him with those innocent eyes. No matter how little he welcomed this news, how angry he was at the woman he'd once loved, he couldn't say anything in front of the child.

He took a breath. "We have to talk."

Miranda turned the child toward the swinging doors. "You go on back to the kitchen. I'll be with you in a little bit."

The boy nodded. After another curious glance at Tyler, he pushed through the door.

He gave the child—his child—another moment to get out of range. He heard the swish of the kitchen door closing. He could speak, if he could find the words.

"Well, Miranda?"

Her soft mouth tightened. "Not here. Anyone might walk in."

The fact that she was right didn't help. His son. The words pounded in his blood. "There must be privacy somewhere in this place."

She gave a curt nod, then led the way to the room on the right of the hall.

Tyler shut the door firmly, glancing around at overstuffed, shabby chairs, walls covered with family photos, a couple of toy cars abandoned on a round pedestal table. He didn't remember being in this room

Indian River Area Library
3546 S. Straits Hwy.

before, but that wasn't surprising. Miranda's family had been as opposed to their relationship as his had been.

He swung toward Miranda.

"Well?" he repeated. "Why did it take you eight years to let me know I'm a father? Or didn't you want child support until now?"

She flinched, her eyes darkening. "I don't need or want anything from you, Tyler."

He suppressed the urge to rant at her. Tyler Winchester didn't lose control, no matter what the provocation. That was one of the keys to his success. "Then why send me that picture now?"

"I didn't!"

Even through his anger, he had to recognize the sincerity in her voice. And he couldn't deny the shock that had been written on her face when she'd first seen him.

"You mean that, don't you?"

She nodded.

"Then who?"

"I don't know. Does it really matter? You know."

"I should have known eight years ago." His anger spiked again. "Why didn't you tell me, Miranda? Even if our marriage was a mistake, surely I deserved to know I had fathered a child."

She crossed her arms, hugging herself. He'd thought, when he first saw her, that she didn't look any older than she had at eighteen. Now he saw the faint lines around her eyes, the added maturity in the way she stood there, confronting him.

Indian River Area Library
3546 S. 2? an? Hwy.

"Well?" He snapped the word, annoyed at himself for the weakness of noticing how she looked.

She spread her hands out. "I don't know what you want me to say, Tyler. By the time I knew I was pregnant, our marriage was over."

He'd told himself he barely remembered that one short month. That wasn't true. He remembered only too well—remembered the furious quarrel with his father over his involvement with a local girl, remembered storming out of the beach house intent on showing the old man that he could manage his own life.

A runaway marriage would do it. He hadn't found it difficult to persuade Miranda or himself that was their only option. They'd come back from their secret honeymoon to face the music—to tell both their families they were married.

Miranda's father had been disapproving but ready to accept the inevitable.

Not his. His father had ranted and raged at both of them, his emotions spilling out like bubbling acid. And then he'd had a heart attack. He'd died before the paramedics reached him.

Tyler slammed the door on that memory. He'd better focus on the present. "You were having our baby. I should have been told."

Anger flared in her heart-shaped face. "You wanted the divorce."

"I had a right to know," he repeated stubbornly. He moved toward her a step, as if he could impel an explanation. But this wasn't the old Miranda, the sweet young woman who'd been so dazzled by love she'd gone along with anything he said.

"What was the point?" She brushed a strand of coppery hair away from her face impatiently. "You were busy taking your father's place and saving the company. You had a life mapped out that didn't include a child."

"And you figured you didn't need me." That was what rankled, he realized. She hadn't needed him then, didn't seem to need him now.

"I had my family."

She gestured toward the groupings of family photographs hung against the wallpaper, the movement sending a whiff of her scent toward him. Soap and sunshine, that was how Miranda had always smelled to him. She still did, and he was annoyed that he remembered.

"They thought you shouldn't tell me?" This branch of the Caldwell clan had never had much money, as he recalled. He'd have expected them to be lining up for child support long before this.

She glanced at him with an odd expression he couldn't quite pin down.

"They were as opposed to our marriage as your family was, remember? They never held with marrying someone from a different world. My daddy said only grief could come from that."

"Looks like he was right, doesn't it?"

Her chin lifted, looking considerably more stubborn than he remembered. "I have Sammy. I don't consider that a source of grief, no matter what."

"Sammy." He didn't even know his son's full name. "What's the rest of it?"

She didn't look away. "Samuel Tyler Caldwell, like mine."

It struck him, then, a fist to the stomach. He had a son. Somehow, he had to figure out how to deal with that.

"Didn't he ask questions about his father?"

She winced. "Of course he asked. Any child would."

"And did you bother telling him the truth?"

"Sammy knows his father's name. He knows our marriage ended because we weren't suited to each other."

It was what he believed himself, but it annoyed him to hear her say it. "Why does he think I never came around?"

"When he asked, I told him you had to work far away." For an instant there was a flicker of uncertainty in her face. "Eventually he stopped asking. He gets plenty of masculine attention. My father, my brothers, my cousins—he doesn't lack male role models, if that's what you're thinking."

It hadn't been, but now that she said it, he knew the sprawling Caldwell clan would take care of its own. But Sammy was his son. He didn't know what that was going to mean yet, but it had to mean something.

"I'm his father."

She crossed her arms again, as if she needed something to hang onto. "He doesn't have to know you were here. You can leave, and we'll go back to the way things were."

"I don't think so, Miranda."

"Why not? You don't want to have a son."

"Maybe not, but I have one. I'm not just going to walk away and pretend it never happened."

She took a breath, and he seemed to feel her gathering strength around her.

"If you mean that, then I'll have to tell him you're here."

His world shifted again. He had a son. Soon that son would know Tyler was his father.

# Chapter Two

Had she ever felt quite this miserable? Miranda sat on the porch swing, staring across the width of the inland waterway at the sunset over the mainland. Maybe, when she was eighteen and discovering that she couldn't function in Tyler's world. And that her fairy-tale marriage wouldn't survive the strain.

At the sight of Tyler standing in the hallway that afternoon, all the pain of losing him had surged out of hiding. Tyler was back—Tyler knew about Sammy. Somehow she had to come to terms with that.

This old swing, on the porch that stretched comfortably across the front of the inn, had always been a refuge. It wasn't today.

She closed her eyes, letting the sunset paint itself on the inside of her lids. *Lord, I don't know what to do.*

No, that wasn't quite right. She knew what she had to do. She had to tell Sammy his father was here, before her son heard it from someone else. She just didn't know how.

*Please, Lord, help me find the words to tell Sammy without hurting him.* Panic gripped her heart. *Don't let Tyler's coming hurt him. He's so young.*

Certainly there weren't any easy words for this situation. Telling her family that Tyler was here had been difficult enough—telling her son would be infinitely worse.

Her mother had been comforting, her father rigidly fair, silencing the angry clamor of her three brothers, who wanted to dump Tyler into the deepest part of the channel. Her sister, Chloe, married now, hadn't been present, but she'd undoubtedly join them as soon as she heard.

Her father had been firm. Tyler had a right to see his son, Clayton Caldwell had said. They'd have to put up with it, for Sammy's sake.

That had been the only thing that would make the twins and Theo behave, she suspected. David and Daniel considered themselves substitute fathers, while Theo had always been a big brother to his ten-years-younger nephew. None of them would do anything to hurt Sammy.

She rubbed her forehead tiredly, then tilted her head to stare at the porch ceiling, painted blue as the sky. She cherished her family, but coping with their reactions had made it impossible for her to work through her own feelings about Tyler's reappearance.

Maybe she wouldn't have been able to, anyway. Just the thought of him seemed to paralyze her with shock.

"Momma?" Sammy pushed through the screen door and let it bang behind him. "Grandma says you want to talk to me."

She forced down a spurt of panic and patted the chintz-cushioned seat next to her. *Please, Lord.*

"Come sit by me, sugar. We need to talk."

Sammy scooted onto the swing. Those jeans were getting too short already, she noticed automatically. He was going to have his father's height.

His face clouded. "I studied for my arithmetic test. Honest."

She was briefly diverted, wondering how Sammy had done on that test. What she had to tell him made arithmetic unimportant for the moment.

"I know you did." She ruffled his hair, and he dodged away from the caress as he'd been doing for the last year or so, aware of being a big kid now. For an instant she longed to have her baby back again, so that she could savor every single experience.

Tyler had missed all those moments. Tension clutched her stomach. Was he angry about that? Or just angry that she hadn't told him about his son?

Sammy wiggled. "Is somethin' wrong?"

"No. I just need to tell you something." She hesitated, searching for the words.

"Somethin' bad?"

Sammy must be picking up on her apprehension, and that was the last thing she wanted. She forced a smile. "No, not bad. Just sort of surprising."

Say it, she commanded.

"You know the man who was here this afternoon, when you got home from school?"

He nodded.

She took a breath. "Well, that was…Tyler Winchester."

Sammy jerked upright on the swing. "My father?"

"Your father. He came to see you."

Her son's small face tightened into an expression that reminded her of his grandfather's when faced with an unpalatable truth. "He never wanted to before."

"Sugar…" He didn't know about you. Her throat closed at the thought of saying that. She ought to, but she couldn't.

"He wants to see you," she said finally. "He wants to get to know you."

Sammy slid off the swing and stood rigidly in front of her, his solemn expression at odds with his cartoon-character T-shirt. "When?"

"Maybe tomorrow after school?" She made it a question. "If that's okay with you."

"I'll think on it." That was what her father always said when presented with a problem. I'll think on it.

"All right." She was afraid to say more.

He went to the door, his small shoulders held stiffly. Then he paused. "Will you come up and say good-night?"

She couldn't let her voice choke. "In a minute."

She watched him disappear into the house. He'd taken it quietly, as he did everything, but this was a bigger crisis than he'd ever had to cope with in his young life. And she was to blame.

Had it really been for Sammy's sake that she'd hidden his existence from Tyler? She struggled to say the truth, at least to herself.

She'd been so distraught when she'd come home from Baltimore, her marriage in tatters, that she hadn't even realized what was happening to her body. By the time she did, she'd already been served with the divorce papers. The trek she'd made to Baltimore in a futile effort to see Tyler and tell him had only convinced her that their marriage was over.

She crossed her arms, hugging herself against the breeze off the water. She'd made her choice. This was the world for her son—the secluded island, the patient pace of life, the shabby inn, the sprawling Caldwell clan who'd accepted him without question as one of them.

Now Tyler was back, with his money and his power and his high-pressure life. He wanted to see his son.

What if he tried to take Sammy away? The question ripped through her on a tidal wave of panic. She wasn't as naive now as she'd been at eighteen, but she still knew that power and money could sometimes overcome justice.

The Winchester wealth might dazzle Sammy. She couldn't compete with all the things Tyler could give him.

Worse, Sammy could risk loving him, as she had. What were the chances Tyler would walk away again, leaving broken hearts behind?

Tyler pulled into the shell-covered driveway of the Dolphin Inn that evening, his lights reflecting from the eyes of a shaggy yellow dog who looked at him as if deciding whether to sound an alarm. His son's dog?

That was one of the many things he didn't know about his child. Maybe that was why he hadn't been able to stay in his room at the island's only resort hotel.

He'd never intended to start a family. The example his parents had set would be enough to sour anyone on the prospect of parenthood. It was too late now. He'd fathered a child.

Deep inside a little voice said, Run. Go back to Baltimore, forget this ever happened.

Tempting, but impossible. Would he eliminate those days with Miranda if he could, even knowing how their relationship would end?

Of course. Their marriage had been a mistake, pure and simple, born out of sunshine and sultry breezes.

He got out of the car, his footsteps quiet on the shell-encrusted walk. The dog, apparently deciding he wasn't a threat, padded silently beside him. He rounded the building and had to force himself to keep walking.

Miranda's family waited on the wraparound porch, at least the masculine portion of it. She'd told them.

Tension grabbed his stomach. They had no reason to welcome him. They couldn't stop him, but they could make this more difficult if they chose.

"Evenin'." Clayton Caldwell didn't offer his hand, but at least he didn't seem to be holding a shotgun.

"Mr. Caldwell." He stopped at the bottom of the

porch steps. "Is Miranda here? I'd like to talk with her." Has she told our son about me?

Miranda's youngest brother shoved himself away from the porch railing. "Maybe she doesn't want to talk to you."

The kid's name floated up from the past. Theo. Theo had the height of all the Caldwell men, even at seventeen or so. Dislike emanated from him.

"That's enough, Theo." Clayton's soft Southern voice carried authority. He eyed Tyler for a moment. "Miranda's down at the dock."

Tyler jerked a nod, then spun away from their combined stares. He walked toward the dock that jutted into the channel between Caldwell Island and the mainland, aware of the men's gazes boring into his back.

Miranda stood with her hands braced against the railing, her jeans and white shirt blending into a background of water and sky. She must have heard his footsteps crossing the shell pathway, then thudding onto the weathered wooden boards. She didn't turn.

Caldwell boats curtseyed gently on the tide on either side of the dock as he approached Miranda. Her slim form was rigid.

Slim, yes, but there was a soft roundness to her figure. The bronze hair that had once rippled halfway down her back brushed her shoulders.

It's been eight years, he reminded himself irritably. Neither of us are kids any longer. If they hadn't been kids, fancying themselves Romeo and Juliet when their families tried to part them, maybe that hasty marriage would never have happened.

Then there'd be no Sammy. The thought hit him
starkly. That would be a harsh trade for an untroubled
conscience.

Miranda turned toward him, her reluctance palpa-
ble. He looked at her without the anger that had colored his image of her earlier.

Her shy eagerness had been replaced by maturity.
She probably had a serene face for anyone but him.

That serenity had been the first thing that attracted
him to her. She'd worn her serenity like a shield even
while she waited tables at the yacht club, taking flak
from spoiled little rich kids. Like he had been.

Just now her body was tight with apprehension, her
face wary. She stood outlined against the darkening
sky, and the breeze from the water ruffled her hair.

One of them had to break the awkward silence.
"Should I have called before I came over?"

She shook her head, the movement sending strands
of coppery hair across her cheek. "It's all right. I
thought you'd probably come back tonight." A ghost
of a smile touched her lips. "We have things to settle,
I guess."

"Yes." He bit back the horde of questions he
wanted to throw at her. Why didn't you tell me? She
still hadn't answered that one to his satisfaction. "I
take it you've told your family."

"I didn't have a choice. You can't come back to a
small place like Caldwell Cove after all these years
and not cause comment. You must remember what
the grapevine is like."

"We were summer people. The island never included us."

Her face shadowed, and he almost regretted his words. Summer people. The wealthy visitors who owned or rented the big houses down by the yacht club had always maintained a clear division between themselves and the islanders.

"I guess not," she said carefully.

"Did you tell Sammy?"

She rubbed her arms, as if seeking warmth. "I told him."

"How did he take it?" He didn't know if he wanted his son to be glad or sorry he was here.

"He was upset. Confused." She shook her head, and he saw the stark pain in her eyes. "I tried to explain."

"I hope you did a better job of explaining it to him than you did to me."

"That's not fair."

"Funny, but I don't feel too much like being fair, Miranda." The anger he'd thought he had under control spurted out. "It isn't every day I find out a girl from my past had a baby she never bothered telling me about."

"I tried to tell you."

He raised an eyebrow. "Tried how? I wasn't that hard to find. A letter or phone call would have done it."

Some emotion he couldn't identify flickered across her face. Once he'd known the meaning of her every look, every gesture. At least he'd told himself he did. Maybe that had been an illusion.

"I came to Baltimore," she said slowly, not looking at him. "Not long after I'd gotten the papers."

He didn't need to ask what papers. His mother had wielded the Winchester clout as easily as his father. She'd pushed the divorce through in record time.

"You didn't oppose the divorce." That wasn't what he'd intended to say, but it just came out.

"No, I…" She stopped, seeming to censor whatever she'd been about to say. "That doesn't matter now."

He leaned against the weathered railing next to her, studying her down-tilted face and wishing he could see her eyes. "If you came to Baltimore, I didn't see you."

"I changed my mind," she said carefully. "I did what I thought was best for all of us. Maybe I was wrong, but it's too late now."

He stared at her, frowning. He wanted to push for answers, but maybe she had a point.

"All right, forget what we did or didn't do then." He didn't think he could, but he'd try. "Let's talk about now. Is Sammy angry about his father showing up after all this time?"

"Not angry, no." Her grip on the railing seemed to ease. "Confused, as I said, but he's a much-loved, secure child. He can deal with this."

None of that love and security in Sammy's life came from his father. Well, fair enough. Tyler hadn't had that from his father, either.

Again he had the urge to walk away. All he could offer this child was money. He'd lost the capacity to form close relationships a long time ago, if he'd ever had it.

He couldn't leave until he'd talked with Sammy. He owed both of them that much, at least.

"When can I meet him?" He threw the question at Miranda.

Her soft mouth tightened. "I suggested tomorrow, and he said he'd think about it. I'd like to let him agree without pressuring him."

Was she trying to get out of it? "I have a business to run, Miranda. Tomorrow after school. I'll be here."

Her head came up, and she glared at him, then jerked a nod. "I'll talk to him about it."

"Tomorrow after school. I'll see you then."

He pushed away from the railing. He'd gotten what he'd come for. He had no reason to linger.

Miranda took a quick step, stopping him. "I said I'd talk to him, Tyler. I'm not going to force him to do something he doesn't want to, just because you're in a hurry."

He swung toward her, and they stood only inches apart. He could read the expression in her eyes—she was wishing for distance between them. He reached out and caught her wrists in his hands, feeling smooth, warm skin and a pulse that thundered against his palms.

"It's already been his lifetime, Miranda. I won't wait."

"Fine." She jerked her hands free, and fierce maternal love blazed in her face. "Just you be careful of what you say to him. If you hurt Sammy, I promise you, I'll make you regret you ever heard of Caldwell Cove."

*  *  *

"Chocolate, vanilla or something more exotic?" Tyler lifted his eyebrow as he asked the question, and Miranda tried not to let that simple movement affect her. She was immune to Tyler Winchester's charm— she'd gotten there the hard way.

She concentrated on the list of flavors posted behind the counter in the ice-cream shop. "I'll have the peanut-butter ripple."

Taking a walk through town with Sammy after school had been her idea. It seemed so much less intimidating than pushing the boy into a face-to-face interview with a father he didn't know.

She'd suggested to Sammy that they show Tyler around Caldwell Cove, not that there was much to see. The village still lay in a sedate crescent along the inland waterway, anchored by the inn at one end and Uncle Jeff's mansion at the other. The spire of St. Andrew's Church bisected the village. Little had changed since Tyler was here last, except for the new resort hotel down near the yacht club.

She had an ulterior motive for this walk. She wanted Tyler to understand that Sammy belonged here. Sammy's happiness didn't depend on anything his father could give him. Maybe when Tyler realized that, he could go away with a clear conscience.

Tyler handed Sammy a chocolate cone, then took a small vanilla for himself. Conservative, she thought. When had Tyler become conservative?

When he'd been drawn back into the Winchester way of life, probably. He'd slipped into his father's place as CEO of Winchester Industries, apparently forgetting that he'd ever had other dreams.

Concentrate on the present, she ordered herself. Don't succumb to the lure of the past.

They stepped onto the narrow street bordered by the docks, and she looked for an inspiration to give them something to talk about.

"Sammy, why don't you tell your father about the boatyard."

Her son didn't seem too enthusiastic about his role as tour guide. He licked, then pointed with an ice-cream daubed finger toward the docks and storage sheds lining the quay.

"That's Cousin Adam's boatyard. He fixed Grandpa's fishing boat when the motor died."

"Adam took all of us on the schooner for Pirate Days, remember?" she prompted.

Enthusiasm replaced the caution in Sammy's face as he turned to Tyler. "That was really cool. I got to help put up the sails and everything. Cousin Adam's going to give me sailing lessons this summer. He says me and Jenny are big enough to learn."

"Jenny is Adam's little girl," she explained. "You must remember Adam, don't you?"

"I remember Adam." His expression suggested the memory wasn't a happy one. "As I recall, he, um—" he glanced at Sammy "—suggested it would be better if I didn't see you."

She felt her cheeks grow warm and hoped he'd attribute it to the March sunshine. "I didn't know that." It made sense. Adam, Uncle Jefferson's older son, belonged to the rich branch of the family, the one that sometimes frequented the yacht club. He would have heard the rumors that his little cousin, who was supposed to be waiting tables at the club, was instead dating a wealthy summer visitor.

"Your ice cream is dripping." Tyler reached out with a napkin and dabbed at her chin just as she ducked away from his touch. His fingers brushed her cheek instead, and her skin seemed to burn where they touched.

"I'll get it," she said hurriedly, hoping the napkin she raised to her lips hid her confusion. She couldn't be reacting to Tyler. She was immune to him. Remember?

"Mine's getting away from me, too." Tyler licked around the top of the cone, where the ice cream had begun a slow trail toward his fingers. "I'd forgotten how hot it can be on the island in March."

"Summer's on its way," she said, then regretted that she'd mentioned the season. Tyler wasn't to know it, but summer always brought back memories of him. She glanced at his face involuntarily, then wondered how often this adult version of her first love indulged in something as simple as an ice-cream cone.

Tyler licked a froth of vanilla from his lips, drawing her gaze. He'd always had a well-shaped mouth. He didn't smile as easily now as he had when she'd known him, and she didn't think that was entirely due to current circumstances. Maybe Tyler didn't find much to smile about anymore.

It probably would be an excellent idea to stop looking at Tyler's lips. Next she'd be remembering how they felt on hers, and things could only get worse from there.

They strolled along the tabby sidewalk, uneven from the shells that formed part of the concrete, worn by a century or two of foot traffic. Live oaks shaded them, and Sammy hopped carefully over a crack in the walk.

Concentrate on what you're doing, she commanded herself. "Don't you want to tell your father about your school?" she asked.

Sammy flicked a faintly rebellious look toward her. "That's it." He waved at the white frame building, set in its grove of palmettos, that had served the island's children for over a hundred years. "I'm almost done with second grade."

"Looks as if the building's been there a hundred years." Tyler said just what she'd been thinking, but it didn't seem complimentary when he said it.

"It's a good school." She hoped she didn't sound defensive. What if Tyler thought his son should go away to some private academy? The idea turned her ice cream to ashes.

"Equipped with the latest in chalkboards, no doubt."

She felt diminished by his sarcasm, and that angered her. "Our classrooms have computers. We're not exactly living in the dark ages here."

"I like my school." Sammy stopped, frowning at Tyler with an expression so like his father's it nearly stopped her heart. "You shouldn't put it down just because it's not new and fancy."

Tyler looked baffled, and little wonder. He probably hadn't expected Sammy to pick up on the byplay between adults.

She was tempted to let him stew, but she couldn't. If she didn't take pity on Tyler's efforts with Sammy, she would only hurt her son.

"Why don't we have a game of catch." She nodded toward the playground where island children had played under the spreading branches of the live oaks for years. "I brought the ball." She pulled it from her bag and tossed it to Tyler, stepping onto the grass.

He caught it automatically. "I don't think…"

She frowned him to silence. Didn't he see she was trying to help him? "Sammy wants to play T-ball this summer. I'll bet he could use some practice."

"Sure. Right." He swallowed the last of his cone and threw the ball to Sammy, then patted an imaginary glove. "Throw it in here, Sammy."

Sammy lobbed it to Miranda instead. She didn't miss the quick flare of irritation on Tyler's face. Well, he couldn't expect this to be simple, could he?

Temptation whispered in her ear again. It would be so easy to be sure Sammy didn't warm up to his father. So easy, and so wrong. Even if it insured that Tyler would go away, she couldn't do it.

Her throw went a little high, and Sammy had to reach for it. He wore a surprised look when he came down with the ball.

"Good catch, Sammy." Tyler's voice had just the right amount of enthusiasm. Sammy responded with a cautious smile.

Tyler blinked, his face softening with the effect of that smile. Her eyes stung with tears, and she was grateful for the sunglasses that shielded them. Tyler didn't need to know that it moved her to see Sammy playing with his father.

That wasn't the purpose of this little excursion, remember? You're supposed to be showing Tyler what a happy life Sammy has here so he'll soothe his conscience and go away.

Tyler's comments about getting back to his business had confirmed what she'd already suspected—he'd turned into the same driven businessman his father had been. She'd known that would happen when he'd insisted they move back to Baltimore after his father's death.

Their dreams of settling down on the island and starting a small business had vanished like the mist. Tyler hadn't had time for that. Now the CEO of Winchester Industries probably didn't like to take time for a simple game of catch.

"Try it this way." Tyler walked over to Sammy, reaching toward him to correct his throw.

Sammy jerked away. "I don't want to."

"Sammy," she began, but what could she say? Be polite to the father you've never seen before didn't seem to cover it.

Her son frowned, first at her, then at Tyler. "Why do you want to play ball now? You never even wanted to see me before."

Miranda's heart thudded. There it was, the question she didn't want to answer. But she didn't have a choice.

She couldn't look at Tyler. She didn't even want to meet her son's eyes, but she forced herself to. "Sammy, that's not fair."

"It is, too." His fists curled. "He could've come, but he didn't."

"No, he couldn't." She felt Tyler's gaze on her.

"Why not?" Sammy demanded.

Truth time was here, and she wasn't ready for it. She had to be. "Your daddy didn't know about you."

Her son stared at her.

She licked dry lips. "I never told your father about you." She reached a hand toward Sammy, but he took a step back. "Sugar, I thought it was best."

The words sounded feeble to her own ears. Hurt and accusation battled in Sammy's face. As for Tyler…she could almost think that was pity in Tyler's eyes.

# Chapter Three

"I have a proposition for you." As soon as the words were out of her mouth, Miranda realized she could have phrased it better. Standing in the doorway to Tyler's hotel room that evening had rattled her so much that she didn't know what she was saying.

"A proposition?" Tyler looked as startled at her words as she probably did. "In that case, I guess you'd better come in."

Clutching her bag with cold fingers, she stepped inside. They could hardly discuss Sammy's relationship with his father at the house, where her son would wonder what they were talking about. Any public place was out of the question.

Tyler crossed the room to switch on another lamp against the darkness that pressed against the sliding glass balcony doors, giving her a moment to collect herself. She took in the sweep of plush, sand-colored carpet, the pale walls and the cream furniture with pastel floral upholstery. Dalton Resorts knew how to treat their wealthy guests.

"I haven't been in the hotel before. It's quite…elegant." It was certainly the antithesis of the Dolphin Inn, but people who could afford this wouldn't be staying at the inn anyway.

Tyler looked at her, hand still on the cream pottery lamp. He had traded the casual shirt and khakis he'd worn for the meeting with Sammy for a white dress shirt, open at the throat, and dark trousers. Maybe the dining room in the hotel required formal attire. Or maybe that was just how he felt comfortable now.

"I thought your brother-in-law worked for Dalton."

"Luke did start out with Dalton, and he helped pick the site for the hotel." Her brother-in-law had been a driven businessman, too, before her sister, Chloe, brought out a different side to him. "He and Chloe are running the youth center in Beaufort now."

"That's quite a change." He strolled toward her, and she had the sense that he wasn't in the least interested in what Chloe and Luke were doing. He was wondering what had brought her here tonight.

"Yes, well, they're happy." Chloe and Luke's love was so bright that it almost hurt to look at them.

Tyler stopped, a bit too close for comfort, and she glanced past him. He'd converted an oval glass-topped table to a makeshift desk. It was littered with papers and centered with a sleek laptop computer.

"I see you've been working."

He followed the direction of her gaze, frowning.

"Business doesn't stop just because I'm out of the office. We have an important deal coming up soon."

The fact that he couldn't even get away from Winchester Industries for two days gave her a surge of confidence. Her plan to deal with this situation was dangerous, but it would work. It had to.

Tyler turned to her, still frowning. A lock of dark brown hair had fallen over his forehead, the only thing even faintly disarranged about his appearance. Had he run his hand through his hair in frustration over being tied here when his business was in Baltimore?

"How is Sammy?"

She took a breath, trying to think of Sammy without pain. She'd let him down so badly.

"He's doing all right," she said carefully. "All this has been hard enough on him, without finding out—" She stopped, started again. "I should have told him the truth about you long ago. I was wrong."

She waited for him to say she should have told him, too, but he didn't. She could almost imagine she saw sympathy in his eyes.

"Do you think he understands why you didn't?"

"I don't know." Sammy's small face appeared in her mind's eye. "As much as an seven-year-old can, I guess. He forgives, even if he doesn't understand."

He studied her face for a long moment, his expression unreadable. "You wanted..." His tone made it a question.

She looked at him blankly, realizing that she'd been staring at him as if she'd never seen him before. Or as if she'd never see him again.

He lifted an eyebrow, something that might have been amusement flickering in his face. "You have a proposition for me, remember?"

"Oh. Yes."

He had to be deliberately attempting to make her nervous. There was no other reason for him to be standing so close, taking up all the air in the room.

Concentrate. This idea will work, won't it? *Please, Lord.*

"You said this afternoon that you want to be a part of Sammy's life." It frightened her just to say the words. "You must realize that you have to get to know Sammy before that can happen."

She expected him to bring up again the fact that it was her fault he didn't know Sammy, but he nodded. "I realize that. I don't want to rush him. But I'm not going to disappear."

She clasped her hands together, trying to find a core of strength inside. "This can't be a halfway thing, Tyler. I won't let Sammy be hurt by it."

"I'm not looking to hurt the boy." He sounded impatient. "So what is this idea of yours?"

Now or never. She had to say it.

"You stay here, on the island, for one month." She swept on before he could interrupt. "You can move into the inn, so you'll see Sammy every day. Then—" She breathed a silent prayer. "Then we can make arrangements together for you to be a real parent to him."

"Stay here?" He made Caldwell Island sound like the outermost reaches of the earth, and his firm mouth tightened even more. "I can't do that. I have a business to run."

That was what she'd thought he'd say, but even so, the words made her heart clench. Tyler would see how impossible this was, that was the important thing.

"I'm not trying to be unreasonable." She nodded toward the computer. "You can stay connected, go back to Baltimore for a day or two if you have to. Surely even the CEO gets some vacation time."

"I can't run a business that way, especially not now." His dismissal was quick. "Sammy can come to Baltimore to get to know me."

Fear flared and had to be extinguished. "Sammy isn't a package, to be sent back and forth when you have time for him. If you want to be his father, you have to realize that. You getting acquainted with him needs to happen here, where he feels safe."

His eyes narrowed. "Suppose I just start legal action. You can't keep me from my son."

The thought of facing a phalanx of ruthless Winchester lawyers made her quake, but she held her voice steady. "And have our private quarrel splashed all over the papers? I don't think you'd like that. And I don't think a family court judge would look favorably on a father who won't take a few weeks to get acquainted with his son."

Something that might have been surprise flickered in his eyes. "You've grown up, Miranda."

"I've had to."

"What you ask is impossible. You must know that."

It wouldn't have been impossible for the man he'd

been at twenty-one, but she couldn't say that, and maybe it wasn't even true. Maybe she hadn't really known the man she'd married.

She had to say the hard thing and end this now, before it damaged Sammy. Tyler's sense of duty to the child he'd fathered had brought him here, but his sense of duty to the company would take him away again.

"If you can't get away from your business for something this important, maybe you're not meant to be a father."

Tyler didn't answer. He couldn't. She had known all along how this would turn out, but still pain clenched her very soul. She turned away.

He grasped her arm, pulling her around to face him. At his touch, her treacherous heart faltered. She forced herself to look at him, her gaze tangling with his. Her breath caught in her throat, and for an instant she thought his eyes darkened.

"I know a challenge when I hear one, Miranda." His voice lowered to a baritone rumble. "I've managed too many business deals not to know when someone's making an offer they think I won't accept."

"I don't—"

His grip tightened. His intense gaze was implacable. "Get a room ready for me. I'm moving in tomorrow."

This was certainly a far cry from the elegance of the Dalton Resort Hotel. Tyler tossed his suitcase onto the patchwork quilt that adorned the four-poster bed in the room to which Miranda had shown him. He glanced around, wondering if he'd made a hasty decision the previous night. Did he really propose to run Winchester Industries from this small room on an island in the middle of nowhere?

He strode to the east window and snapped up the shade, letting sunlight stream across wide, uneven floorboards dotted with oval hooked rugs. Someone had put a milk-glass vase filled with dried flowers on the battered, rice-carved bureau, and the faint aroma seemed a ghost of last summer's flowers.

Well, there was a phone jack, at least. With that, something to use for a desk and enough electrical outlets, he ought to be able to make this work if he wanted to.

Maybe that was the question. Did he want to do this? He frowned at what seemed to be a kitchen garden. The small patch of lawn, crisscrossed with clotheslines, couldn't be intended for the use of guests. Beyond it was some sort of shed, then the pale green-gold of the marsh grasses. A white heron stood, knee-deep, waiting motionless for something.

Tyler assessed his options, trying to weigh them as if this were any business deal that had come up unexpectedly. In a business deal, the first step would be to research what was being offered. He grimaced. Miranda wasn't exactly offering him anything. As for research—well, he didn't need a DNA test to confirm what he knew in his bones. Sammy was his son.

He could stay. That meant subjecting himself to the uncertain welcome of Miranda's family and trying to figure out how to be a father under Miranda's no doubt critical gaze. Then, assuming he could gain Sammy's acceptance, he'd face the tricky task of working out long-distance custody arrangements between Baltimore and Caldwell Cove and he'd commit himself to being a significant part of Sammy's life for—well, forever.

He shoved the window up, letting the breeze that bent the marsh grasses billow the ruffled curtains. The alternative was to leave. Go back to Baltimore, take up life as it had been. He could afford generous child support, the best schools, anything material his son needed. He could satisfy his conscience without getting emotionally involved.

"Is everything all right?" Miranda paused in the doorway, clutching an armload of white towels against the front of a green T-shirt with a dolphin emblazoned on it.

No, Miranda, nothing's been all right since that photo of Sammy landed on my desk. Miranda was undoubtedly talking about the room, not his inner struggle.

"Fine."

"You looked as if you might be having second thoughts about this, now that you've seen the accommodations." She put the towels on the edge of the bureau.

"The accommodations are fine."

"If you want to change your mind—"

"I don't," he said shortly, trying to ignore the fact that he'd been thinking just that. He'd better concentrate on the room instead of noticing how well those faded jeans fit her slim figure. "I need something to use for a desk. A table would work, if you have one to spare. If not, I'll go out and buy one.''

''No need. I'll find something.''

She shoved a strand of hair from her eyes. He found himself thinking that its color was nearer mahogany than auburn and then told himself that it didn't matter in the least what color Miranda's hair was. She vanished before he could say anything, her quick footsteps receding down the hallway.

All right, he needed some rules if he were actually going to stay here. The first one had to be no staring at Miranda. And the second one better be no remembering the past.

He heard her coming before he could decide on rule three. Something thumped against the wall. He reached the door to see Miranda backing toward him, holding one end of a rectangular oak table. Her mother, wearing a dolphin T-shirt also, wrestled with the other end. He sprang to help them.

''Mrs. Caldwell, let me take that.''

Sallie Caldwell surrendered her grip, giving him a smile too like her daughter's for comfort. ''I'm afraid the table doesn't match the rest of the furniture, but Miranda said that didn't matter.''

Miranda had probably said that if he didn't like it he could lump it.

''It'll work.'' He guided the heavy table through the doorway, finding it necessary to remind himself again not to let his gaze linger on Miranda's face. Her cheeks were slightly flushed, either from exertion or because she had indeed said what he imagined.

Miranda helped him position the makeshift desk

near the window. Then, as if she thought she'd spent enough time in his company for one day, she retreated to the doorway where her mother waited.

"If there's anything else you need, just let us know." Sallie Caldwell put her arm around her daughter's waist with easy affection as she smiled at him. She had Miranda's bronze hair, streaked with gray.

"I will." He tried without success to imagine his mother letting gray appear in her hair or wearing faded jeans and a T-shirt.

"We'll try to make you comfortable while you're here."

They all knew there was nothing comfortable about any of this. Still, he sensed that Miranda's mother meant what she said. There was no artifice about her—just the same unselfconscious natural beauty her daughter had.

"Thank you, Mrs. Caldwell. The room will work just fine."

If I stay. The words whispered in his mind as the Caldwell women vanished down the hall.

His cell phone rang, and he flipped it open. Probably Henry, responding to the message he'd left at the office. But it wasn't his assistant—it was his brother.

"Henry's secretary passed your message on to me. He's out of the office. What's going on?" Curiosity filled Josh's voice.

"Out of the office where?" What was reliable Henry doing out of the office when he'd left him in charge?

"Didn't tell me." He could almost see Josh's

shrug. "Something you want me to take care of before he gets back?"

His first instinct was a prompt no, but someone at the office had to know where he was. And why. And how long he intended to stay.

"Not exactly." He hesitated. His brother would have to know. As irresponsible as Josh was, he wouldn't spread the news if Tyler asked him not to. "I have a…situation here, and I don't want anyone else to know the whole story. You can tell Henry, but no one else. Understood?"

"Got it." He could almost see Josh leaning back, propping his feet on the desk. "What's up?"

"You remember Miranda Caldwell?"

A pause, but Josh would remember. After all, their father's death had rocked both their worlds.

"Your ex-wife."

"Yes. Turns out there was something she neglected to mention when we got divorced. I have a son." He waited for an explosion of questions.

Instead Josh whistled softly. "I assume you're sure he's yours."

"I'm sure."

"What are you going to do about it?"

The very question he'd been asking himself. Apparently he already knew the answer. "I'm going to stay here for a while to get to know him."

He expected an argument. He didn't get it. "Okay. I'll tell Henry. What about Mother?"

"Not yet." He thought uneasily of their mother, honeymooning in Madrid with her new husband. She wouldn't be happy that Miranda was back in his life. "Thanks, Josh."

He hung up, realizing why he didn't want to tell anyone. The possession of a son had made him vulnerable. He didn't like to be vulnerable. Miranda's image presented itself in his mind and refused to be dismissed. Look where vulnerability had gotten him eight years ago.

Several hours later, he sat back in the chair and stretched, congratulating himself. He had a reasonable facsimile of an office set up, he'd been in touch with Henry about his plans and he'd contacted the Charleston subsidiary of Winchester Industries and arranged a meeting there, since it was only a couple of hours away. Almost as much as he might have accomplished in Baltimore.

At corporate headquarters, though, he wouldn't have been quite so distracted by the view from the window. There, he'd look out on the Inner Harbor. Here, he looked out at Miranda, busy putting sheets on the clotheslines strung across the yard.

He stood, frowning at the photo of Sammy he'd propped next to his computer. The reason had nothing to do with sentiment, he assured himself. He'd put it there to remind himself that he had to find out who'd sent it, and why.

He picked it up, gaze straying again to Miranda. The chances he'd learn the truth about that without her help were slim and none. Therefore he needed to enlist her aid. He glanced at his watch. He'd better do it now, before Sammy came home from school.

Tucking the photo into his shirt pocket, he headed for the backyard and Miranda.

When he pushed open the screen door, Miranda was bending over an oval wicker clothes basket. She looked up at the sound, and her face went still at the sight of him.

"I thought you were busy with work." She shook out a damp sheet and began pinning it to the line, as if to show him that she was busy, as well.

"I've made a good start." He approached her, then had to step back as she shook out another sheet. "Don't you have a dryer?"

"Of course we have a dryer." At his raised eyebrow, she shook her head as if in pity. "We like to sleep on air-dried sheets. So do our guests."

"Why?" He caught the end of the sheet she was manhandling. For a moment he thought she'd yank it free, but then she handed him a clothespin.

"They smell like sunshine."

You smell like sunshine. He dismissed the vagrant thought. "Wouldn't it be more efficient to use a laundry service?"

"That's not how we do things here." She snapped out the words as if he'd insulted her. Sunlight filtered through live oaks and dappled her face.

He reminded himself that he wanted her cooperation, not her enmity. "So you're helping to run the inn now."

"That's right." She pinned up another sheet. "My college plans were derailed."

She'd been saving money that summer, he remembered, waiting tables at the yacht club so she could attend the community college that fall. Both their lives had gone in an unexpected direction, but hers had obviously been skewed more than his.

"I'm sorry," he said, and meant it.

She looked at him for a long moment, then nodded in acceptance. "I don't regret anything." A smile blazed across her face. "I have Sammy."

He nodded, the photo seeming to burn a hole in his pocket. Maybe he'd better get to the point before he brought up any more touchy subjects. "I've been thinking about that picture of him."

"I've already told you, I didn't send it." She snatched the basket and ducked under flapping sheets to the other end of the yard.

He followed, evading damp linen. He needed her on his side in this. "I know you didn't send it. Don't you want to know who did?"

"Yes, of course." She stopped, eyes clouded. "I've worried and worried, and I still don't have an idea."

"There has to be a way to find out. Why don't we talk to Sammy about this?"

"Absolutely not." She shot the words at him, shoulders suddenly stiff.

"But he may have noticed who took the picture."

"I mean it, Tyler." Her soft mouth was firm. "I don't want him questioned about this."

"That's ridiculous. If we can find out—"

"It's not ridiculous," she snapped. It looked as if they were back on opposite sides. "If we talk to Sammy, he's going to ask how you got a picture of him."

"We can say—" He stopped. What would they say?

"I don't want him thinking that some stranger is going around taking pictures of him, manipulating his life." A shiver seemed to run through her. "It's bad enough thinking that myself."

"All right."

Miranda looked at him suspiciously, and he raised his hands in surrender.

"I promise. I won't say anything to him."

The tension went out of her, and she reached up to unpin a dry sheet. He caught the end of it, and she let him help her fold it.

"Why? That's what gets me," she said. "Why would anyone want to interfere in our lives like that?"

"I wish I knew." He had to hurry to keep up with the deft way she flipped the corners together. "No one's said anything to you about it?"

"Nothing."

He finished the last fold, then put the sheet into the basket as Miranda moved on to the next one. She was right—the sheet did smell like sunshine.

"Stop a minute and look at it again." He drew the photo from his pocket and handed it to her.

She studied the picture, absently twisting a strand of hair around her finger. Her gaze lifted, startled, to him. "This looks like—"

"What?"

"Come with me." She dropped a clothespin into the basket and started around the inn at a trot. He had to hurry to keep up with her.

"Look." She stopped at the corner of the veranda, pointing.

He stepped closer, looking over her shoulder at the photo, then at the scene in front of them. An ancient, gnarled live oak filled the corner of the yard, its branches so heavy they touched the ground in places. From this angle, they formed a kind of archway through which he saw a corner of the dock. It was exactly the same in the photograph.

"Whoever he was, he took the picture here," he said.

This time he was so close he felt the shiver that went through her.

"Here. And sometime within the last six months." She touched the photo with one fingertip. "I bought that polo shirt for Sammy when school started in September."

"Stands to reason it was fairly recent. If he wanted to send it to me, whoever he was, why wait?"

Miranda's breath seemed to catch. "Tyler, we have to find out who did this." She swung around, apparently not realizing how close he was. She was nearly in his arms.

He caught her arm as she bumped against him. Her smooth skin seemed alive with memories—visions of holding her close, of promising to love her forever. The fresh scent of her surrounded and overpowered him.

This was bad. This was very bad. He'd never dreamed those feelings still existed, ready to be awakened. It was as if the very cells of his body remembered her.

He'd wanted Miranda's cooperation. He'd gotten it, but in the process he'd found out something very unwelcome about himself. He was still attracted to her.

# Chapter Four

Miranda couldn't move. Tyler held her elbows, steadying her, and her hands pressed against his chest. She felt his heartbeat through her palms, up her arms, driving straight to her heart. It had been years since they'd stood together like this. It might as well have been yesterday.

She curled her fingers, pulled her hands away from him. She couldn't look at his face. Instead she focused on the placket of his white knit shirt. Two of the three buttons were open, exposing a V of tanned skin against the white.

That wasn't any better than looking into his eyes. She took a hurried step back, and he released her instantly. If he guessed her reactions—

He wouldn't. Tyler was too focused on the task at hand to have time for any other considerations. At the moment he was totally consumed with finding out who'd taken the photo of Sammy.

She wanted to know that, too, but somehow she

also had to find a way of keeping her balance where Tyler was concerned. That meant not finding herself in any more moments like that one.

Tyler glanced from the photo to the scene before him. He frowned, and she sensed that, as far as he was concerned, the moment when they'd touched might never have been.

Well, good. That was what she wanted, too.

"So, we know the picture was taken within the last six months, and by someone standing in just about this spot." He seemed to measure the distance from the driveway to the street. "How unusual would it be for someone you don't know to come this far onto the property?"

She steadied herself. Tyler didn't feel anything. She wouldn't feel anything, either.

"Not unusual at all, I'm afraid."

"Why not?" He shot the question at her with that intent, challenging stare of his. "If someone's not a guest at the inn, why would he be here?"

She pointed to the small placard attached to a post near the end of the driveway. "The historical society put those up a few years ago. I worked on the project, as a matter of fact. We designed a walking tour of historical houses. Visitors can pick up a brochure anywhere in town and follow it. In nice weather we often see people, brochure in hand, taking pictures."

"There's no way of tracing them?"

"None. People don't buy tickets or sign up. They just follow the map." A shiver ran along her arms, and she rubbed them. "Sammy wouldn't think anything about it, even if he noticed someone with a camera.'' She took another step away from him. "I should get back to the laundry."

"Wait a minute." His hand twitched as if he thought about touching her and changed his mind. "We haven't finished talking about this."

"I don't know how to find the person who took the picture. There's nothing else to say. I want to take down the sheets before it's time to start dinner." And I want to put a little distance between us.

"Fine." He seemed to grind his teeth. "I'll help you with the sheets, if that's what it takes. We can talk and fold at the same time."

She's forgotten how persistent he could be when he wanted something. "Sammy will be home in a few minutes. I don't want him to hear anything about this."

He slid the photo into his pocket. "I've already said he won't hear it from me, Miranda." He moved past her, then stopped and raised an eyebrow when she didn't follow. "Aren't we going to fold laundry?"

Without a word, she brushed past him and started around the house, aware of him on her heels. Persistent. Aggravating. Determined to have his own way. Tyler hadn't changed—those qualities had intensified, probably from years of surrounding himself with people who always agreed with the boss. Well, he'd have to get used to the fact that this situation was different.

She reached the dry sheets she'd hung out earlier and began taking them down. Tyler let her get one more sheet into the basket before he started in again.

"There's no reason to suppose it was a stranger, anyway."

She frowned at him, not sure where he was going with this.

He frowned back. "Well, think about it, Miranda. Why would a stranger go to the trouble of taking a picture of Sammy? How would a stranger even know who he was? Or who his father was?"

Good questions, all of them. Unfortunately, she didn't have any good answers. She turned it over in her mind as she took a pillowcase off the line.

"I suppose it might be some bizarre string of co-incidences. Weird things do happen. Someone visiting the island to whom your name would be familiar, maybe, then finding out about Sammy."

It sounded weak to her. Judging from Tyler's expression, it sounded pitiful to him.

"I don't believe in that wild a coincidence." He unpinned a sheet and handed her one end, his fingers brushing hers. "How widely known is it that I'm Sammy's father?"

The only surprising thing was that he hadn't asked the question sooner. "Islanders know, for the most part." She carefully didn't look at him. "Our elopement was quite a sensation. People talk."

"Gossip." He sounded uncompromising.

"Talk," she said again. "But folks here are used to the situation. I don't think they'd mention it to outsiders, anyway. Islanders protect their own."

"Unless there's something in it for them."

She didn't know how to combat that kind of cynicism. "You're wrong, Tyler. No one here would deliberately set out to hurt me or Sammy."

"Then what's left?" His brows twitched, impatience returning. "I can't believe in some kind of random coincidence. You can't believe your neighbors would meddle. What are we left with? Your family?"

"No!" She planted her fists on her hips. "Tyler, that's ridiculous. No one in my family would do anything like that."

"According to you, no one would do it, but it happened." He ducked under the clothesline, and it brushed the top of his head. The movement brought him within inches of her, and her breath stuttered.

"Get rid of your rose-colored glasses for a minute, Miranda. Someone did this thing. Someone deliberately took a picture of Sammy and sent it to me. Someone who knew I was Sammy's father and knew how to reach me."

His words battered her like waves in rough surf. She brushed her hair from her eyes, looking at him.

"Why?" The word came out in a whisper. "Why, Tyler?"

He caught her hands, imprisoning them in his hard grip. "We'll find out, but you have to help me. We can't be on opposite sides in this."

Opposite sides. The only safe place for her was not opposite, but as far away from Tyler as possible.

His grip tightened, compelling a response. "You have to help me," he repeated.

The more she was near him, the more difficult and dangerous it would be to her heart. She didn't have a choice.

"All right. I'll help you."

* * *

"Tyler, would you like another piece of fried chicken?" Sallie Caldwell held the platter out to him. It had been piled high with golden chicken pieces when they sat down, but one trip around the table had diminished it considerably.

"No, thanks, Mrs. Caldwell. I have plenty." He'd already made his way through two pieces and a mound of mashed potatoes and gravy. He hadn't eaten like this since—well, he'd never eaten like this.

The long table, set in the center of the dining room, was used as a buffet for guests' breakfasts, but now light from the overhead fixture fell on seven Caldwells and one unwelcome guest.

Miranda's mother must have her hands full, cooking for this bunch every day. David and Daniel, seated opposite him, were a couple of years older than Miranda. Both tall and lean, they wore the same stamp their father did of men who worked hard in the outdoors. People like that didn't need to worry about getting to the gym to work off an extra serving of fried chicken.

Theo, the baby of the family, alternated between focusing on his plate and glaring at Tyler. He was clearly not reconciled to Tyler's presence at the family table.

Nobody was, he supposed. Sallie had a smile for him, but that was either her natural expression or her idea of Southern hospitality. Sammy fidgeted in the ladder-back chair that was a little too big for him, probably eager for the Friday night movie Miranda had said he'd be attending with his cousins.

Tyler could feel Miranda's tension from across the table. He knew its cause. They'd agreed that once Sammy was off to the movies, she'd talk to her family about the photograph.

She didn't want to do it, didn't think it was necessary. He crumbled a feathery-light biscuit between his fingers. She'd only agreed because she'd known that if she didn't, he would.

Talk of the weather shifted to fishing. Tyler's gaze crossed Miranda's, and she glanced quickly away. Was she disappointed at his silence? She must realize that he didn't have much to say on either subject. He wasn't going to try to manufacture conversation with his son while all of them listened.

Not that Sammy seemed to notice. He avoided Tyler's eye, piping into the conversation about fishing once or twice. He said something teasing to one of his uncles about coming home with an empty net and earned a grin and a ruffle of his hair.

"Did I tell y'all I saw the pod today?" That was David, he thought, though the twins were so alike it was hard to tell.

"Sure that wasn't a sand shark?" His twin's voice was lazily teasing. "Or maybe an old inner tube?"

"Did you honest, Uncle David?" Sammy bounced on his chair. "You should've taken me out with you. I'm good at spotting them."

"School first, then dolphins," David said easily. "How'd you do on that spelling quiz?"

Sammy sent an uneasy glance toward his mother. "Okay, I guess."

"Just okay? Maybe we better drill a bit more this week."

"My turn to help Sammy this week," his twin interrupted. "I'm a better speller than you ever thought of being. Isn't that right, Momma?"

Sallie turned that hundred-watt smile on him. "Funny, that's not how I remember it. Maybe I ought to get out your old report cards. Let Sammy see how his uncles did in school."

Good-humored protests from the men vied with Sammy's cheers at the idea. Tyler leaned back. He wasn't part of the circle of Caldwells around the table. Whether meaning to or not, they'd made that clear to him.

His childhood table hadn't borne much resemblance to this. His parents, before they divorced, dined in the elegant room with the crystal chandelier and the velvet drapes. He and Josh had a nursery supper, he supposed, but then he'd been shipped off to boarding school, where supper was a noisy affair with people who weren't related to you.

Was that the kind of childhood he wanted for Sammy? He looked at the boy, smiling at some quip his grandfather had aimed at the twins. The laughter in his son's eyes was for the Caldwells, not for him.

Something Miranda had said about Sammy being a well-loved child rang in his mind. Sammy had plenty of people to love him. Miranda had plenty of people to support her. It didn't look as if either of them had any need of him.

Headlights flashed against the windows, and a car horn sounded. Sammy was off his chair in a flash. ''That's my cousins, Momma. Can I go now? Please?''

''Not with chicken on your mouth.'' Miranda handed him a napkin, and he mopped his face quickly.

''Now?'' His feet moved as if he were already running.

''All right.'' Miranda grabbed him before he could dash. ''But you say goodbye properly first, y'hear? And don't forget to mind Cousin Matt.''

''I won't.'' Sammy planted a quick kiss on Miranda's cheek. ''Bye, Momma. Bye, y'all.'' His gaze, rounding the table, came to Tyler and stopped.

Tyler could almost see the thought running through his son's mind. Sammy didn't know what to call him.

''G'night,'' he muttered. Then he dashed out the door.

Clayton's children, though grown, called him Daddy with open affection. Tyler's son didn't have a word for him. That mattered more than he'd have expected.

''Before y'all go, there's something I want to ask you.'' Miranda clearly didn't like it, but she intended to fulfill her promise.

David, who'd half stood, sat down again. ''What's up, sugar?''

''Y'all know about the picture of Sammy someone sent to Tyler.''

There was a murmur of assent and one or two hostile glances sent his way.

"We...I feel like I need to know how that happened. So I'm asking for the truth. Does anybody know anything about it?"

Tyler's fists clenched under the edge of the woven tablecloth. If they did, would they admit it?

For an instant her family stared at Miranda without speaking. Then Theo smacked his palm against the table. "No! You can't think we'd do anything to bring him here."

Clayton cleared his throat. "No need to get riled, Theo. The thing's worrying at her, and your sister's got a right to ask." He looked around the table, his clear glance seeming to measure each of them in turn. "Anybody know anything about this?"

The anger faded from Theo's face, leaving him looking young and vulnerable. "No, Daddy."

"No," the twins said together.

Sallie shook her head.

"Nor I," Clayton said. He reached across to clasp Miranda's hand. "I understand why you wanted to ask, sugar. Anybody thinks of anything that might help, you tell Miranda right off." He pushed his chair back. "Mind, now. Anything at all."

That seemed to be a sign of dismissal. The family filtered out of the room until only Tyler and Miranda were left. She began stacking plates on top of one another, as precisely as if it were crucial that they lined up evenly.

Finally she looked at him. "They were telling the truth."

"I know." He did know. Whoever had sent that

photo, for whatever reason, it wasn't one of the people who'd sat around the table tonight.

"They'd never do anything to hurt me or Sammy." She said it as if she expected an argument.

He had none to make. They loved her. They'd supported her and Sammy for the past eight years, when he hadn't been a part of their lives.

They didn't need him. Neither the woman he'd once loved nor the son he hadn't known about needed anything he had to offer.

Had Tyler believed her family? Miranda shoved the tip of the spade into the soft earth at the corner of the front porch the next morning, her mind far from the azaleas she meant to plant.

He'd said he did. She frowned at the sandy earth she'd turned. Her people hadn't sent Tyler the photo of Sammy. They wouldn't. Probably next he'd want to ask her sister, then her cousins, then anyone else he could think of.

Her thoughts touched on an army of Caldwell second cousins and courtesy aunts. Everyone knew who Sammy's father was, but they'd all known for her son's entire life. If they'd wanted to make trouble, they could have done it any time in the last eight years.

She leaned on the shovel for a moment, glancing past the crepe myrtles that edged the yard. Sammy was at the dock, spending his Saturday morning helping David clean the boat. He could have been doing something with his father, but Tyler was upstairs in the room he'd turned into a branch office of Winchester Industries.

The really exasperating thing was the fluctuation of her feelings about that. One minute she wanted to pressure him into spending time with Sammy, the next she assured herself that it was better this way.

You're a mess, she told herself sternly. Decide what you want and stick to it.

That was certainly one of those things easier said than done. *Lord, maybe You'd better show me what I'm supposed to do in this situation, because I surely can't figure it out for myself.*

The screen door banged, and she heard footsteps on the porch.

"Are you digging or daydreaming?" Tyler leaned on the porch rail.

"Digging." She shoved the spade in and struck a root. "We had a lilac bush here, but it died, so I'm putting in some azaleas." She nodded toward the pots behind her. "My brothers have been promising to dig the bed for me, but they always have something more important to do."

Tyler came down from the porch as she spoke. Before she knew what he was about, he'd grasped the spade.

"What are you doing?" Her grip tightened.

He lifted an eyebrow. "Isn't that obvious? I'll do the digging for you."

"I can do it myself." Amazing how childish that sounded.

"I'm sure you can." The look he gave her suggested the words meant more than the obvious. "I'd

Indian River Area Library
3546 S. Straits Hwv.

like to help you, however, and you wouldn't be so impolite as to refuse.''

She let go of the shovel and moved out of his way. ''My momma taught me never to be rude.''

Tyler shoved the spade into the earth, striking the same root she'd hit.

''I guess I should have mentioned that the old roots from the lilac were still there.''

He maneuvered the blade underneath the root, prying it up. ''Guess you might have.''

He'd left her with nothing to do, but she could hardly walk away. It would be better if she didn't stare quite so obviously at the movement of his muscles under the white knit shirt he wore.

She picked up one of the potted azaleas. ''Looks like that hole's about ready for the first one.''

Tyler moved back to give her room, then knelt beside her to help slide the azalea from its pot into the hole. Together they pressed the earth around the plant.

''How long has it been since you've gotten your hands dirty like this?'' She tamped the soil down with a trowel.

He shrugged, so close she felt the movement brush against her. ''A while, I guess.''

It was too bad Sammy wasn't here to see his parents working together on something. That might be better for him than constantly sensing their tension. But Sammy was off with his uncle because his father had had something more vital to do with his Saturday morning.

''Did you finish up whatever work was so important this morning?'' She didn't mean her question to sound quite as condemning as she feared it did.

Tyler's expression told her he'd taken it that way. ''I have a business to run, remember?''

''Don't you take Saturdays off?''

''Maybe, when I haven't spent Wednesday, Thursday and Friday on other things.''

''Important things.'' Like your son, for instance.

He leaned on the shovel, studying her face for a moment. ''Is it important for you to help your family run the inn?''

The question took her by surprise. ''Yes, but…that's different.'' It was, wasn't it? ''That still leaves me plenty of time for Sammy. Besides, my family depends on me.''

''The people who work for Winchester Industries depend on me. I try not to let them down.''

That was probably true, though she couldn't help but believe his devotion to his position was more consuming than it had to be.

''Can't your brother take some of the load?'' Josh had still been in school when she and Tyler were married, but she remembered it had been assumed he'd go into the company, too. That was what Winchesters did.

''Josh doesn't handle responsibility very well.'' Tyler began digging the second hole with unnecessary force.

She sat on her heels, watching him. ''Doesn't he also work for the company?''

Tyler's face set. ''If you call having a corner office

with his name on the door working for the company, I suppose he does.''

''Don't tell me there's a Winchester who'd rather do something else.'' She said the words lightly, but a chill touched her. Was Tyler thinking that now he had a son to fill the role Josh apparently didn't?

''Josh talks a good game.'' He grabbed an azalea and shoved it into the hole. ''But when I trusted him with something important to do, he let me down. I won't make the same mistake again.''

Tyler's expression was as impervious as granite. His brother had let him down, and he didn't forgive that.

Her chill intensified. Tyler didn't forgive. No matter how they managed to cooperate about Sammy, she'd best keep one thing in mind. Tyler would never forgive her for not telling him about their son.

# Chapter Five

Tyler tamped the earth around the last of the shrubs, then stretched. His back felt tight from the unexpected labor, but it was a good sensation. He hadn't done any physical work outside the gym for a long time.

"Is that it? Or are you hiding some more plants somewhere, just waiting for someone to come along and help you?"

"That's it." Miranda sprinkled pine bark mulch around the bushes, then smiled at him. "Thanks, Tyler. I really didn't expect you to do this."

"I know. You could have done it yourself." He followed her to the hose. She sprayed sun-warmed water over his hands.

"I could have." A note of defensiveness touched her words. "You didn't have to leave your work on my account."

Was that a slap at him for working this morning instead of doing something with Sammy? He took the hose from her, holding it so she could wash her hands.

She hesitated for a moment, then thrust her hands under the spray. Small hands, but strong and capable, like the rest of her.

He frowned, trying to look honestly at his actions over the last few hours. What he'd said to Miranda was true—he did have work to do, and he didn't trust his brother to take over for him.

Unfortunately, a niggling conscience suggested that hadn't been the only reason he'd hurried to his room after breakfast. Had he been backing off from spending time with his son, avoiding a possibly awkward encounter with Sammy?

If so, he had to do something about that, and quickly. His only reason for being here was to build some sort of relationship with his son.

Miranda turned off the hose, coiling it against the latticework beneath the porch. She had to be wondering what was going on with him. Trouble was, he didn't know.

"Is Sammy still down at the dock?" he asked abruptly.

She nodded, a question in her eyes. "He's helping David clean the boat."

"Maybe I'll see if he'd like to do something with me." Like what? He hadn't a clue.

"I'll walk down with you."

Miranda fell into step with him as he crossed the lawn, then the shell-covered path. Was she thinking he needed her intervention with Sammy?

Sunlight sparkled on the waterway between the island and the mainland. A sailboat dipped and swayed in the wind as gracefully as a dancer. Gulls circled the mast, white against a sky that was bluer than it could ever be in the city.

The weathered wooden dock stretched into the water, lined with boats on either side. He stepped onto it, his gaze held by the sight of a small figure industriously polishing the chrome trim of a white catamaran. His son. A feeling he didn't recognize welled inside him.

"They're cleaning up the *Spyhop*. David uses her for the dolphin watch, and Daniel takes visitors out on her."

"Sammy likes doing that?"

The wind ruffled Miranda's hair into her face and fluttered her oversize blue T-shirt. "He loves it." Maternal pride blazed in her eyes. "He's turning into a real waterman, just like his grandfather and uncles."

Not like his father, in other words. She seemed determined to turn the boy into a complete Caldwell with no trace of Winchester to be found. That bothered him more than he'd expected.

Miranda stopped level with the boat. "Hey, guys. You've got the *Spyhop* looking like new."

"Not quite that." David ran a paper towel over the windscreen. "But I'd say she's ready for the season. Sammy's been a big help."

Sammy's gaze slanted off Tyler and landed on his mother. "I did all the polishing."

Tyler seemed to feel an invisible push from Miranda, demanding that he respond. "Good job."

"Thanks." Sammy hesitated, as if on the verge of saying his name, then let it trail off.

Tyler braced himself against the railing, the rough

wood warm under his hands. He had absolutely no reason to be nervous about this. If he could walk into a multinational corporation's boardroom as if he owned the world, he could surely invite a seven-year-old to spend some time with him.

"Sammy, I thought maybe you'd like to run into town with me." He felt ridiculously like a teenager asking for a first date. "We could stop and get a hamburger for lunch if you want."

For a moment no one moved or spoke. A gull squawked above them, and he sensed Miranda holding her breath. What was she wishing for?

His son squared his shoulders as if facing something unpleasant. "I already promised to go on a dolphin watch with my uncle. But thank you."

Miranda's hand clenched on the railing next to his. "Sammy, you can go on the next trip. I'm sure Uncle David wouldn't mind."

"That's right," David began, but Sammy shook his head, his mouth setting stubbornly.

"We just got the boat ready. I want to go today."

"Fine." Tyler hoped that didn't sound as curt as he feared it did. "We'll do it another time."

"Maybe you'd like to go along on the boat," Miranda said quickly. "They have plenty of room."

"No, thanks."

Miranda meant well, but he had no desire to compete with David for Sammy's attention. He stepped back, watching as Sammy loosed the lines that held the *Spyhop* to the dock. His son moved around the boat easily, as if advertising the fact that he was at home there.

The catamaran nosed slowly through the water away from them. Sammy hopped onto the seat next to his uncle, and David let him put his hands on the wheel as they steered into the current.

"Tyler, I'm sorry."

Was she? "Leave it, Miranda. Sammy can do something with me another day."

Everyone wants something from you. Here was one case where his father's prediction had been wrong. Miranda hadn't wanted anything from him but out. It appeared Sammy was felt exactly the same way.

She should be glad Tyler wasn't fitting in. Miranda had been telling herself that for the past hour, but if it were true, why did her heart ache for both Tyler and Sammy?

She pulled the car into the drive next to the church, got out and unloaded the bucket of red tulips and yellow daffodils from the back seat. Maybe a little time spent alone in the sanctuary while she arranged the flowers for tomorrow's service would help calm her mind.

*I don't know what to do, Lord. I don't even know how to pray in this situation. Maybe You'd best give me some direction, because I'm sure not doing very well on my own.*

She straightened, closing the car door, and heard someone call her name. Gran Caldwell waved from the front porch of the white clapboard house next to the church where Caldwells had lived for the past hundred and fifty years or so.

"Miranda, come along over here. I've got some lilacs for the vases."

Miranda picked up the bucket and started toward her grandmother, her steps making little sound on the thick carpet of pine needles.

"Hey, Gran. I already have some of Momma's tulips and dafs." She hefted the bucket as she grew near, hoping she could keep the conversation on flowers instead of the tangle her life was in at the moment.

"No paperwhites?" Gran did love the pale, old-fashioned cream narcissus. "We'll cut some of those, too, with the lilacs."

Miranda followed the spare, erect figure in the faded print dress along the hedge of lilacs—deep purple, pale lavender, pure white. Her grandmother's green thumb was legendary. She inhaled, the perfume taking her back to playing under the lilac hedge with her sister, Chloe, on warm spring afternoons that seemed to last forever.

How long would it take Gran to bring up Tyler's arrival? Not long, she'd guess.

Gran cut a spray of purple blossoms with her shears and turned it in her hands as if assessing its worthiness to appear in the church vases. Then she looked at Miranda, her faded hazel eyes still sharp even though she'd soon celebrate her eighty-first birthday.

"I hear Tyler's back on the island."

"Yes." No sense trying to avoid discussing it with Gran, even if she wanted to. Gran always knew everything that happened on the island, and she generally knew what you should do before you did. "Someone sent him a photograph of Sammy."

"So he came. Well, I reckon that's what he ought to do."

"Ought to do?" She set the bucket down. "Gran, he's furious that I never told him about Sammy."

Her grandmother eyed her sternly. "I'm not saying his coming here is a good thing. I'm just saying if he's any kind of an honorable man, he'd have come once he found out about the boy."

Honorable. Tyler's face filled her mind, and she felt the jolt to her heart that she should be getting used to by now. Honorable wasn't a word she associated with Tyler, but maybe Gran had a point.

"I guess it might have been easier to toss the picture away and tell himself it was some sort of joke." But then, Tyler never had been one to do things the easy way.

Gran nodded. "He wouldn't do that, not if he was a man you could have fallen in love with." She snipped another stem of blossoms. "How is it going?"

Miranda thought about Tyler's rigid figure as he watched Sammy go off on the boat with David. "Not well." She tried to swallow, but there was a lump in her throat that wouldn't go away. "He and Sammy— they just seem to glance off each other instead of connecting. Maybe that's best, anyway."

"Best? Way I hear it, you were the one who asked Tyler to stay. Now you wanting him to leave?"

"I didn't think he'd agree." Her reasoning seemed vaguely shameful when she tried to explain it to her grandmother. "I thought he'd say he was too busy and that would make him see that he didn't have time for Sammy. I thought he'd go away, and we could go back to our lives."

"And now that he's staying, seems like everything's changed."

All the things she hadn't been able to say to anyone else began to pour out of her mouth. "Gran, I just don't know what to do. If they go on the way they are, Tyler and Sammy are never going to be anything to each other. But if I help them…"

Her voice choked. Gran folded strong arms around her, holding her close. Miranda inhaled the lavender scent that always meant Gran to her.

"There now, child. Did you take it to the Lord?"

Miranda nodded, trying to sniff back tears. "I've prayed about it and prayed about it. I don't know if it's better for Sammy to lose his father now or to try and divide his life between our world and Tyler's. I guess the truth is, I'm scared."

Gran took Miranda's face between her hands, her palms dry and cool against Miranda's flushed cheeks. "Seems to me you're trying to push God into choosing between your two options. How do you know the Lord doesn't have something else in mind entirely?"

"But—what else is there?"

"Miranda Jane Caldwell, you took vows before God to love that man forever. Did you ever think maybe God wants the two of you back together again?"

For an instant she could only stare at Gran's face. The world narrowed to the question that hung in the air between them, Gran's challenging gaze, the faint buzz of a bee investigating the lilacs.

"That's impossible." The words came out forcefully. She took a step back. "Gran, that can never happen."

"Why not?"

"Isn't it obvious?" It certainly was to her. "Even if I wanted that, Tyler certainly doesn't. He's turned into a man just like his father, obsessed with business and making money. I can't ignore that, and even if I could, I still can't be the wife Tyler needs. I couldn't eight years ago, and I can't today."

"You stop that kind of talk." Gran shook her finger at Miranda as if she were six instead of twenty-six. "How do you know you're not the wife Tyler needs?"

"I tried!" Tears stung her eyes at the memory of those humiliating days. "I couldn't fit into Tyler's world. As soon as he saw me there, he must have known that."

"So you came back here, where you felt safe." There was no condemnation in her grandmother's voice, just concern. She took Miranda's hands in both of hers. "Child, you remember the verse I gave you?"

How could she forget? Gran gave each of her grandchildren a Bible verse to live by. Miranda's was embroidered on cream linen, framed and hanging on her bedroom wall.

*Therefore, as God's chosen people, holy and dearly loved, clothe yourselves with compassion, kindness, humility, gentleness, and patience.*

"I remember." She tried for a watery smile. "I'm not sure I do so well with the patience part."

Gran shook her hands as if she'd like to shake Miranda. "You're right good at humility, child. But it seems to me you're forgetting about how God dearly loves you. If you really believed that, you'd know you're worthy wherever you are, whether it's here or in that big house of Tyler's up north."

It was as if she'd looked straight into Miranda's heart. Gran patted her cheek. "You think on that. God will give you the answer. You just have to listen."

She managed to nod, hoping she could somehow hide her feelings from Gran's sharp eyes. She couldn't let herself believe that Gran's idea had any merit, because if she did, she might start hoping for something with Tyler that was never going to happen.

Miranda tucked a spray of white lilac into the vase with the tulips and assessed the effect. Yes, that was going to look lovely.

She took a breath, letting the peace of St. Andrew's seep into her troubled spirit. The small chapel had stood on this same spot for nearly two hundred years. She looked around at the simple wooden pews, the white walls, the stained-glass windows with their colors glowing in the afternoon sunlight. She could use a little peace after listening to Gran's upsetting ideas.

Her gaze was drawn to the image of the risen Christ looking at Mary Magdalene, kneeling before him in the garden. The Christ figure glowed with light, seeming to radiate peace and understanding.

Miranda slipped into a pew, putting her hands on the wooden seat back in front of her and leaning her face against her hands.

*Father, I don't know what to think. Is Gran right? Have I been hiding?*

She longed to reject the thought, but Gran knew her as well as anyone.

*I want to be the person You expect me to be. If I have been hiding, please help me see what to do about it.*

No immediate answer leaped into her mind, but that didn't matter. The answer would come. She had confidence in that.

She stood, feeling better than she had since the moment she'd seen Tyler standing in the hallway, and returned to the flowers.

Half an hour later, she'd finished the two vases that stood on either side of the communion table and begun work on the arrangement for the bracket behind the pulpit. One of the double doors at the rear of the sanctuary swung open, letting in a shaft of sunlight. Tyler walked toward her.

*Please, Lord,* she murmured silently.

"Your mother told me you'd be here." He came to a stop a few feet from her. "She said you were arranging the flowers for tomorrow's service."

Miranda gestured with the narcissus in her hand. "As you can see." She hesitated, not sure she wanted to ask him what he was doing here.

"Very nice." He touched the delicate blossoms of the white lilac. "Where will this one go?"

"There." She nodded. "On the dolphin shelf."

Anyone would think Tyler was here for no other reason than a casual conversation with her. Anyone would be wrong. Tyler never did anything casually.

He moved toward the shelf, his long stride bringing him within inches of her. "Wasn't there some old family legend about that?"

"Yes."

He stopped, looking at her with a raised eyebrow. "Just yes? You could tell me about it, you know."

He almost seemed to be teasing her, and she didn't know how to react. It didn't help that her heart was thumping at his nearness.

"A wooden statue of a dolphin once stood there, carved by the first Caldwell on the island." She mentally deleted all the references to the special blessings that were supposed to come to those wed under the dolphin's gaze. Tyler didn't need any reminder of weddings. "It disappeared a long time ago, when my father was a teenager." Tyler also didn't need to know how her father and uncle had been entangled with that disappearance.

"But you still put flowers on the shelf."

Unnerved by his closeness, she jammed a tulip into the arrangement too hard and broke the stem. "Yes, we do. And I need to get on with it."

Tyler shrugged. "Don't let me stop you."

She could hardly say the truth—that his very presence was enough to disrupt just about anything she might be doing. He moved away, and she could breathe again.

"I'd forgotten how peaceful this place is." He walked toward the side of the sanctuary.

She ought to be able to concentrate on the flowers now that he was at a safe distance. Instead her senses followed him, informing her when he stopped and what caught his attention.

With jerky movements she tucked the rest of the paperwhites into the vase and lifted it to the shelf. There, it would have to do. She could come in early in the morning and adjust it if she had to. At least then Tyler wouldn't be around to distract her.

"This is new, isn't it?" Tyler had stopped in front of the stained-glass window depicting a dolphin surging from the water.

"Yes."

Again he lifted his eyebrows, and again she knew she was being ungracious. It was a bad sign that Tyler brought out the worst in her. Unwillingly she crossed the sanctuary to stand on the opposite side of the window from him.

"It's the Caldwell dolphin. My cousin Adam's fiancée designed and made it."

Tyler touched the crest of a glass wave. "It's beautiful. She's a skilled artist."

"Tory brought back our dolphin, in a way." Things had come full circle. Tory's mother had caused the loss of the dolphin, but Tory had created this beautiful tribute in its place.

Miranda felt Tyler's gaze on her face as she stared at the dolphin. Why had he followed her to the church? She wasn't sure she wanted to know.

"Your family must be very pleased with this."

It was certainly easier to talk about the window than about the situation between them. "We are. Although I think Gran still believes the original dolphin will come back someday."

"Hardly likely after all this time, is it?"

"No, I guess not." *You came back, Tyler. What am I going to do about it?*

She took a breath, summoning her courage. Tyler had something on his mind besides the Caldwell dolphin. She'd better try to find out what.

"Why did you come here looking for me?" It sounded blunt, but it was the best she could do. "Did you want something?"

Tyler's chiseled features seemed to tighten. "I want to talk with you about Sammy."

She saw again his expression when Sammy had gone off with David that morning. Tyler probably didn't experience rejection very often. She suspected he didn't know how to cope with it.

"What about Sammy?"

He moved restlessly, the colored light from the window touching his cheek, then his shoulder. "The point of my staying here is for us to get acquainted. That's a little tough to do when he doesn't want to spend any time with me."

There were a lot of answers to that—that Sammy didn't want to, that she wasn't going to force him, that there wasn't anything she could do.

Gran's words echoed in her mind. If what Gran said was true, it was time she did something about it. No more hiding. She couldn't run from the pain of what she and Tyler had once had. She could only try to repair the damage she'd done when she'd kept Sammy from him.

"It's hard," she said, not sure whether she was talking about Sammy or herself.

"Most things that are worthwhile are hard." His face was uncompromising. "I don't plan to give up on this, Miranda."

Where was the courage Gran insisted all Caldwell women had? Maybe it had skipped her.

"I think it might be best if we planned to do some things with Sammy together." She didn't know she was going to say it until she heard the words come out of her mouth. She'd asked God to show her what to do, and He had immediately given her an opportunity to find out. She couldn't back out now.

Tyler's gaze seemed to probe for the truth beneath her skin. "The three of us together."

She forced herself to meet his eyes. "That will be easier for Sammy."

"It won't be easier for you, will it?"

For an instant she thought she saw sympathy in his face. She must be mistaken. Tyler could hardly feel sympathy for the woman who'd wronged him in such a fundamental way.

"Maybe not. But it's the right thing to do."

He gave a curt nod. "Very well, then." He seemed to slip into his businessman persona. The brief flicker of feeling vanished.

That was for the best. She was only going to get through this if she didn't have too many more disturbing glimpses of the man she'd once loved.

# *Chapter Six*

This wasn't exactly what he'd thought Miranda meant about spending time together with their son. Tyler sat at the round oak table in the parlor on Sunday night with Sammy opposite him, homework spread out between them. Sammy looked as doubtful as Tyler felt about his ability to help with homework.

"How about a snack to help the studying along?" Miranda put a tray down between them. "Do you have a lot for tomorrow?"

Sammy brightened a bit at the sight of oatmeal cookies and milk. "Just my report."

Wonderful. What did Tyler know about the kind of report a second grader would write? He didn't even remember second grade. This evening was out of tune with his normal life as the rest of the day had been, including sitting in church with the Caldwell clan and enduring a huge family dinner.

Sammy bit into an oatmeal cookie and smiled at

his mother. His son, it seemed, smiled at everyone but him. For Tyler he always had a wary look.

Well, maybe homework help was the route to a smile. "What's your report about?"

Sammy flattened a lined yellow sheet on the table. "I'm s'posed to write a whole page about the dolphin from the church. And draw a picture, too."

"That doesn't sound too hard. Your mother told me a little bit about the dolphin yesterday."

Sammy picked up his pencil, then put it down again. "I don't know what to put in and what to leave out."

"Why don't you just talk about it first," Miranda suggested. "Tell your father the story."

Sammy heaved a sigh, prompting an involuntary smile to Tyler's lips. Homework reluctance didn't seem so far away, after all.

"Gran says the first Caldwell on the island made the dolphin," Sammy began. He slanted a look at Tyler's face. "Did you know he was in a ship-wreck?"

"I don't think I heard that part."

Sammy nodded. "Maybe it was even a pirate ship."

Miranda's eyebrows lifted. "Now, you know that's not true."

"It'd be a better story if it was a pirate ship."

"Maybe we ought to stick to the facts," Tyler said. "What did your great-grandmother tell you about it?"

"He was almost ready to drown when he was saved by Chloe and her dolphins." Sammy clearly thought a pirate ship would be more exciting. "Gran always says he took one look at her and loved her.'' He wrinkled his nose. ''Mush.''

''He took one look and knew he'd love her forever,'' Miranda said, her mouth curving softly.

Tyler felt an unexpected, unwelcome tenderness at the sight and had to beat it down. ''I don't think Sammy wants to include the mushy part.''

''True love isn't mushy.'' Miranda looked ready for a fight.

''It is when you're seven,'' he said.

They looked at each other over their son's head, Miranda's eyes very bright. Then she shrugged, long lashes sweeping down to hide the green. ''I guess you can just say he carved the dolphin for the church as a way of thanking Chloe and the dolphins for saving him.''

Miranda obviously preferred the more romantic version. Had she ever told him that story when they were dating? Somehow he thought he'd have remembered if she had. He took one look and knew he'd love her forever.

''Okay.'' Sammy picked up his pencil. ''I can do that.''

Miranda crossed to the shelves that covered one wall. ''I'll find you a picture of the dolphin.'' She knelt, sliding a fat leather album from a whole row of similar albums. ''It should be in here.''

She brought the book to the table and began looking through it. For a few minutes there was no sound but the scratching of Sammy's pencil and the ruffle of pages as Miranda leafed through the album.

It should have been boring, but instead Tyler felt

oddly relaxed. Maybe this was the way he'd envisioned his life for those few summer weeks when he thought he'd found the love of a lifetime—the shabby, comfortable room, the boy's intent face, the gentle curve of Miranda's cheek.

"Here it is." Miranda shoved the album across the table to Tyler, and he and Sammy leaned close together to look at it.

The dolphin was pictured on the shelf he'd seen in the church, against a white wall. Probably an expert would say the carving was crude, but emotion radiated from the form as the dolphin arced upward.

"I can draw that." Sammy pulled a sheet of plain paper toward him. "I've seen lots of dolphins."

Tyler propped the album page in front of him, then slid a book behind it to give Sammy a better angle. His son glanced up with a tentative smile.

"Thanks."

The smile, slight though it was, reached straight for his heart. He glanced at Miranda to find her watching them. She looked down quickly but not before he caught a glimpse of tears in her eyes.

The image was oddly disturbing. Was Miranda that moved to see his son warming to him? Or was she upset at the thought that he and Sammy might find some common bond?

"You know what I think?" Sammy's crayon paused on the dolphin's back.

"What?"

"I think the dolphin's hidden someplace."

Tyler glanced uncertainly at Miranda. She'd said

the dolphin disappeared. Tyler had the impression she didn't believe it would ever turn up again.

"Sammy, I don't think—" Miranda began.

"I do." Sammy touched the faded photograph. "Somebody hid it, and Gran would be really happy if we found it for her." He gave Tyler a questioning look. "I want to look for it. You wanna help me?"

He could practically hear Miranda's thoughts. She didn't want him to encourage Sammy's search. She thought it futile, and she was probably right. But the first time his son asked something of him, he wouldn't say no.

"I'd like that, Sammy. It sounds like fun. Almost like a treasure hunt."

Sammy's blazing smile grabbed his heart and squeezed it. "Okay. We'll find it. You'll see."

Miranda was undoubtedly going to tell him how wrong he was to encourage Sammy in this. He didn't care. Any amount of censure was worth it for that small step into his son's life.


"That's enough chapters for tonight." Miranda put the book on Sammy's bedside table. She knew stalling when she saw it. Even Tyler, standing behind her, probably recognized that. "Prayers now, and then into bed."

Sammy seemed to calculate whether he ought to push for more, then slid to his knees on the rag rug next to the brass single bed that had been his since he'd outgrown his crib. He folded his hands to recite the Lord's Prayer, proud that he'd outgrown the simpler prayers she'd taught him when he learned to talk.

''And please God, bless Momma, and Grandpa and Grandma and Gran, and my aunts and uncles and cousins.'' There was a hesitation, so slight she wondered if Tyler, lingering in the doorway, noticed it. ''And my father. Amen.''

Sammy hopped into bed, pulling up the patchwork quilt Gran had made for him. '''Night, Momma.'' He paused again, his gaze not quite meeting Tyler's. '''Night.''

''Good night, sugar.'' She tucked the quilt over him and bent to kiss his forehead, glad he hadn't outgrown good-night stories and kisses yet. ''Sweet dreams.''

''Good night, Sammy.'' The low rumble of Tyler's voice set something vibrating inside her.

This was like those dreams she'd never shared with anyone—herself and Tyler looking at their son, telling him good-night. In that dream she could feel his solid presence near her, sense his support in all the troubling questions about how to raise a boy to be a good man.

A dream, just a dream. It was as unreal as all those other dreams she'd had over the years of Tyler holding her hand when Sammy was born, standing proudly beside her at the baptismal font, clapping when Sammy recited his verse at the Christmas pageant. None of them were real.

A spurt of panic touched her. Tyler must never know she'd spent the past eight years dreaming he was here with her.

She walked from the room, hearing Tyler's footsteps behind her. Just dreams, except that now they were coming true in a skewed, hurtful way.

Tyler followed her into the parlor. It was still empty. The rest of the family had apparently decided she and Tyler needed time alone to settle things. They were right.

"About looking for the dolphin," she began, turning to face him.

His eyebrows lifted. "You don't like the idea. Why?"

There were too many answers to that. Maybe she'd best stick with the easiest one. "Because it's hopeless."

"Most treasure hunts are. That doesn't mean they're not fun."

"If Sammy sets his heart on finding the dolphin for Gran, he'll be disappointed."

Tyler frowned. "Being disappointed is part of life, Miranda. Sammy can learn to cope with that."

"Are you telling me how to be a mother?" Better to be angry with Tyler than think about foolish dreams that would never come true.

"I'm stating the obvious. No reward comes without risk."

Like the risk she'd taken when she fell in love with Tyler? She pushed the thought away. "That may be true, but there are things about the dolphin's disappearance you don't know."

Tyler propped his hip against the round table, folding his arms across his chest. "If it's something Sammy knows, maybe you'd better tell me, unless it's a family secret."

*You were my husband, Tyler. You had a right to know any of my family secrets.*

She'd better tell him before he said something he shouldn't out of not knowing. "The dolphin disappeared when my daddy and his brother were teenagers. Turns out Uncle Jefferson took it from the church out to Angel Isle to impress a girl—a rich summer visitor. They were all at a party there. The girl's father and his friends raided it. I guess he didn't like his daughter associating with people like us."

That hit too close to home, and for a moment she couldn't go on. Did Tyler see the parallels between that old story and the way his family had reacted to their runaway wedding?

"What happened to the dolphin?" Tyler, frowning, seemed to be focused on the disappearance. Apparently she was the only one who related it to their personal story.

"There was a lot of confusion, and my daddy was hurt in an accident. By the time anyone looked for it, the dolphin was gone."

"So she took it away." Tyler came to the obvious conclusion.

"That's what Daddy always thought, until the woman's daughter came to the island. Tory—the one who made the dolphin window in the sanctuary. She says her mother never took it off the island. It just vanished that night."

"Sammy must think it's still on Angel Isle."

He said the name easily, as if it were just any spot, instead of the place where they'd spent their honeymoon before coming back to face the music with their families.

"I suppose so." She tried to say it with as much unconcern as he did. "I'm sure that's where he wants to look."

Tyler pushed himself away from the table, the movement bringing him close enough she could smell the musky aftershave that clung to him. "Nothing you've told me seems a good enough reason for denying Sammy the pleasure of hunting for it."

"All right. Fine." She turned away, picking up the photo album to return it to the shelf. Anything to put a few feet between her and Tyler. "We'll look for the dolphin." *And I'll try not to remember what Angel Isle once meant to us.*

"You have more of those."

She couldn't imagine what he was talking about. Then she realized he meant the photo album.

"A whole shelf of them."

"Including pictures of Sammy." There was an edge in his voice, but she thought it overlay longing.

"Yes. Of course." She slid the old album into its place and touched the ones that chronicled Sammy's life—three fat albums stuffed with photos of all the things Tyler had missed. Would they make him hate what she'd done even more? Maybe that wasn't possible.

She pulled the albums out and carried them to the table. "Here they are."

Tyler slid into the chair in front of them, then looked at her, a challenge in his dark eyes. "Don't I get a guided tour of my son's life?"

The lump in her throat threatened to choke her. She nodded, sat down and opened the first album.

"This is the day he was born." Her fingertips touched the picture of a red-faced infant, squalling his indignation at being thrust into the world. "It's a little blurry. Daddy took it through the glass of the nursery window."

Tyler pulled the album closer, his hand brushing hers and sending a shaft of awareness along her skin. "Your family was with you."

"Naturally." Did he think they'd have deserted her because she'd come home pregnant and divorced? "Momma was my labor coach. She said it was harder to do than to have all five of hers."

Tyler's hand stilled on the page. "I should have been there."

"You..." She caught the words that wanted to be spoken.

*I dreamed you were there, Tyler. You held my hand, and I saw the incredible joy in your face when our son was born.*

"What?" He turned, his face too close to hers.

"Nothing." Where was this going? Panic ricocheted through her. How could she ever get out of this situation without her heart shattering into a million pieces?

Tyler leaned forward on the bench seat of the catamaran the next afternoon, watching Miranda ease the boat to the dock at Angel Isle. She had suggested they wait until Saturday for this trip, but Sammy had been so eager she'd finally agreed to come today after school.

His son stood on the opposite seat, rope in hand, ready to tie up. Tyler resisted the impulse to grab the back of Sammy's shirt as he reached for the post. He wouldn't appreciate being treated like a baby.

Sammy made the rope fast, then scrambled off to loop the stern line around another post. His movements were as quick and efficient as any sailor's.

"Good job."

His son gave him a smile that seemed a little easier today. Because he was feeling more comfortable around Tyler or because he'd succeeded in getting them to take this trip to Angel Isle today? Tyler didn't know him well enough to be sure.

That added to the list of things he didn't know about this child of his. Resentment had bubbled beneath the surface since they'd looked at those photograph albums.

Sammy, tiny in his grandfather's hands, sitting up in a high chair, reaching for a rattle held by one of his uncles, showing two teeth in a proud grin. He'd missed his son's babyhood, his toddler years. All those landmarks would never come again.

Miranda climbed lightly out of the *Spyhop,* and he followed her, carrying the picnic basket her mother had thrust on them as they went out the door. Apparently Sallie thought they couldn't make the trip without sustenance, even though Miranda had insisted they'd be back for supper.

He patted the pocket where he'd put his cell phone and intercepted a quick glance from Miranda.

"Couldn't leave it behind?"

"Never," he said firmly. "It's permanently attached."

She started up the path, resting her hand on Sammy's shoulder. It was an automatic gesture, one he hadn't quite had nerve enough to make with the boy yet for fear Sammy would pull away.

The resentment burned again as he followed them. Only one thing had kept him from lashing out at Miranda the night before when he'd looked at the photographs of all he'd missed in his son's life. It continued to keep him silent.

Miranda's devotion to their child shone so brightly that a blind person could see it. She'd been wrong not to tell him about her pregnancy, but he had to admit, to himself if not to her, that she'd been trying to do what she thought was best for their son.

Miranda and Sammy paused at the bend in the path, waiting for him under a live oak, its branches festooned with Spanish moss. "Is something wrong?" She pushed bronze curls from her face.

"No." He couldn't tell her he'd lagged behind because he'd been trying to figure out what kind of relationship they could have after everything that had happened between them.

"We're almost there," Sammy said. He darted ahead. "Come on and see the cottage."

He heard the quick catch of Miranda's breath.

"He doesn't know I'm not a stranger here, does he?" he said, and watched the color rise in her cheeks.

"I've never found it necessary to tell him we came

here on our honeymoon, if that's what you mean.'' Her mouth was set firmly. "Did you think I should?''

For an instant he wanted to say something hurtful, something that would pay her back for all he'd missed. He shook his head. "I don't want to fight with you, Miranda.''

Her chin came up. "Don't you?''

"No. Not that I'm not tempted, but I remember what it's like to have parents who hated each other. I won't show Sammy the kind of relationship they had.''

She seemed to digest that for a moment. "I don't see any reason we can't try to be—'' she paused as if searching for the right word "—friendly.''

"Come on!'' Sammy shouted impatiently. "Don't you want to start looking?''

"We're coming,'' Miranda called. She looked as if she would say something more, then turned and went quickly up the path.

He followed, rounded the bend and came to a halt. The cottage stretched in front of them, its porch reaching out welcoming arms across the front of the gray shingled building. He'd carried Miranda up those steps, across the porch, laughing and kissing at the same time.

Miranda glanced at him. "Is something wrong?''

"No.'' He hurried to catch up with her, and they went together up the steps to the porch where Sammy waited, dancing with impatience. Nothing was wrong except that he'd suddenly been slapped with a whole raft of memories he didn't know what to do with.

Miranda seemed oblivious to the effect the cottage

had on him. She took the key from the nail above the door and unlocked it. Sammy rushed in, and she crossed to the windows to throw open the shutters, letting sunlight stream across the wide pine floorboards and touch the hooked rugs and faded chintzes.

"I'm going to look upstairs. Maybe it's hidden in one of the closets." Sammy scrambled up the open stairway.

Tyler stood in the doorway, watching Miranda. They'd married in a tiny church miles away on the mainland, and she'd wept a little afterward because she hadn't been married in her own church. He'd held her in his arms and kissed the tears away.

They'd rented a boat and come here, to the place she loved, for their stolen honeymoon. He'd carried her over the threshold he stood on now, laughing and triumphant. Had that triumph been for marrying the woman he loved or for outwitting their families? He tried to look rationally at the kid he'd been at twenty, but he couldn't.

Emotion had clouded his judgment then. He pushed away from the doorjamb and crossed the room to help her with the shutters. He wasn't a kid any longer. He had to concentrate on establishing, if not a friendship, at least a truce with Miranda. Maybe that was the best they could hope for.

Miranda thumped a recalcitrant shutter with her fist. "This one always sticks."

He grabbed the handle and pulled. With a creak of hinges, it grumbled open.

Sunlight crossed Miranda's face, bringing out the gold flecks in her eyes. She smiled, pushing back the opposite shutter. "You're just trying to make me look bad."

An answering smile touched his lips. "I'd never do that." He brushed her cheek with his fingertips. "Never."

Her hand was arrested on the shutter, as if she'd forgotten she held it. Her eyes met his, wide and questioning.

What was he doing? That had to be the question in her mind, just as it was in his. Surely his brain had a coherent answer somewhere, but it had gotten lost in a flood of memories and feelings brought on by this place, this woman.

"Tyler..."

His name came out on her breath. He cupped her cheek with his hand. Her lips were only inches away. And then he kissed her.

Crazy, crazy, something in his brain shouted, but he wouldn't listen to it. Miranda was as warm and sweet as he remembered, and he didn't want to listen to logic or reason, not now.

He released her mouth, pressed his cheek against her hair. The words came before he thought. "What happened, Miranda? What happened to us?"

# *Chapter Seven*

All the wounded places in Miranda's heart were flooded with a warm, healing light. She'd waited for Tyler's kiss during the long, arid years. Now, with this one meeting of lips, hearts had met, too.

No, oh, no. She drew back, slowly and painfully, feeling as if she were wrenched away and had left her heart behind.

She couldn't make the same mistake again. They'd been down this road together before, and it had ended in unimaginable pain. They couldn't repeat that.

She took a step away from him, knowing the light from the window showed him every expression on her face. Her longing must be written there for him to see, but she couldn't let that matter.

"I'm sorry," he said at last, his dark eyes masking whatever he felt. "That shouldn't have happened."

"No." She cleared her throat and tried to steady her voice. "You asked what happened to us, but we both know the answer to that. If we'd been right for each other, we wouldn't have parted. We'd have fought for our marriage instead of giving up at the first obstacle.''

His mouth tightened. ''We were certainly too young to make lifetime decisions.''

''Yes.'' She tried to smile. ''Very young, and in too much of a hurry.'' She thought of her younger self, crazy in love and longing to be Tyler's wife. She'd thought marriage was the one thing that would guarantee she'd never lose him. Instead, it had driven them apart.

''I would have stayed with you, you know.'' Tyler's dark brows drew down over his eyes, making him look formidable. ''If I'd known about the baby, I'd have tried to make it work.''

Because of Sammy, he'd have tried to make a go of something that would have made both of them miserable. Even knowing how badly things had turned out between them, she couldn't help but wince at that.

''I intended to. But when I came back to Baltimore—''

His mouth hardened. ''I think I can guess. My mother intercepted you, didn't she?''

She nodded. Repeating the cruel things his mother had said wouldn't do any good.

''We can't go back and rewrite the past.'' She took a step back. ''All we can do is try and make things as right as possible for our son.''

He nodded, his face bleak. ''Friends, I think you said. I guess we'd better try.''

He didn't look as if the prospect gave him much joy, but then she could hardly expect that it would.

"Isn't anybody going to help me hunt?" Sammy's plaintive voice floated down from upstairs.

"I'll go," Tyler said. He crossed the room with quick strides and hurried up the steps as if he couldn't wait to be away from her.

She rubbed her arms, cold in spite of the warmth of the day. Tyler had taken all the sunshine out of the room with him, leaving only a gray, draining chill that seeped into her bones and made her feel as old as Gran.

She forced herself to walk across the room and unpack the picnic basket Tyler had left on the round oak table. Lemonade in a jug, red Delicious apples, a bag of oatmeal chocolate-chip cookies—comfort food, and she was certainly in need of comfort. Maybe her mother had guessed that was how it would be, coming back with Tyler to the place where they'd been so happy.

She glanced up when she heard thumps coming from upstairs. They must be pulling things out of the storage spaces beneath the eaves.

The light chatter of Sammy's voice mixed with the deeper chime of Tyler's answers. Sammy was getting past his reserve where his father was concerned. She closed her eyes, groping in prayer.

*Lord, at first all I wanted was to get rid of Tyler, but now I see that's not right. Like it or not, Sammy needs to know his father. I'm trying not to be a coward about this, but I surely could use Your help.*

Some of the tension eased out of her in the silence, and she could look at the situation with more clarity. At some level Tyler must still be attracted to her, but he obviously didn't feel that marriage was forever. If he did, he'd never have agreed to the quick divorce his mother had pushed through.

So she had to find a way, for Sammy's sake, to keep things at a calm, friendly level between them. Committed as they were to spending time together with Sammy, that wouldn't be easy, but it had to be done.

One thing she could never do was betray to Tyler the fact that, for her, marriage was forever. She'd never stopped feeling married to him, no matter how many legal documents or miles or years stood between them. She'd never stop feeling that, but it would be a disaster to let Tyler suspect such a thing.

By the time she'd found napkins and glasses and spread the red-and-white checked cloth over the table, Tyler and Sammy came down the open stairway. One look at Sammy's face told her they'd found nothing.

"No luck?"

He shook his head, his mouth set in a determined line. "But there's lots more places to look. We can't give up yet."

"How about a little snack before you search some more?"

"Sounds good," Tyler said, as easily as if he hadn't been kissing her only a little while earlier.

Sammy slid onto a chair and picked up a cookie. "We went way back under the eaves, Momma. I found a box of old cars. Do you think we could take them home?"

"Why don't you bring them down and put them in

the game room closet instead. Then you can play with them when your cousins are here.''

Sammy nodded reluctantly. ''Guess that would be okay.''

''You come out here a lot, do you?'' Tyler glanced from her to Sammy as he asked the question. Was he remembering when they'd come alone to the cottage, heady with their new status as man and wife?

''Lots in the summer,'' Sammy answered. ''Gran says when Great-grandpa was little, they used to stay out here all summer long. Wish we could do that.''

''We have the inn to run now,'' she reminded him. ''Besides, if we did that, you couldn't play T-ball in the summer.''

Sammy nodded, then cast a sideways glance at his father. ''First practice for T-ball is tomorrow after school. We're s'posed to bring a parent. You could go, if you want.''

''I'd like that,'' Tyler said. He reached out a little tentatively to ruffle Sammy's hair. ''I'd like that a lot.''

She'd been right. Sammy was adjusting to Tyler. She blinked. Both of them would be embarrassed at the idea that they'd brought her to tears.

An electronic peal startled her. ''What was that?''

Tyler reached for his pocket. ''Cell phone. Never go anywhere without it, remember?'' He pulled the phone out, and with it came a square of paper that fluttered to lie, face up, on the floor. It was the photograph of Sammy.

For a moment Tyler froze, not sure what to do. He'd agreed to Miranda's decision that Sammy not be told about the photo. She'd probably assume he'd done this deliberately.

The phone buzzed again, and he snapped it off. He reached for the picture, but Sammy had already grabbed it. Over their son's head he met Miranda's gaze and mouthed a quick sorry.

"Hey, where'd you get this picture of me?"

Sammy looked at him, and the lie that had been tentatively forming in his mind died. Whatever he told his son, it couldn't be a falsehood.

"Well, I..." Okay, where were the words? He didn't have this much trouble dancing around an unpalatable truth in a business deal. Which just went to prove that he was better off avoiding emotional entanglements.

"Someone sent the picture to your father." Miranda didn't seem to have his difficulty in coming out with the truth now that she'd been forced into it. He could read the worry she was trying to hide.

Sammy frowned at the picture. "You mean that bird-watcher guy sent it to you?"

"What bird-watcher guy?" He addressed the question to Miranda, but she looked as perplexed as he felt.

"You know, Momma." Sammy dropped the photo on the table. "That guy who stayed at the inn a while ago. He had those neat binoculars he let me look through."

"You mean Mr. Dawson."

"Yeah, him." Sammy turned away, losing interest. "I'm gonna look in the closets where the games are."

"Just a minute." Miranda touched his arm, stopping him. "Are you sure Mr. Dawson took this picture?"

He nodded. "One day when I got home from school. He said he wanted to finish up a roll or something." He shrugged. "He said he'd give me the pictures, but he never did. Can I go now?"

"Okay." Miranda managed a smile, but her eyes were troubled. "You put all those games back when you're done, though, hear?"

"I'll be there in a minute to help you." As soon as he'd found out what Miranda knew about this Dawson character.

But she got in with the first question as soon as Sammy had disappeared. "Do you know him?"

"I know a lot of people, but nobody called Dawson comes to mind. What did he look like?"

And why didn't anybody notice him taking pictures of our son? That probably wasn't a fair question. This was Caldwell Island, where no one thought twice about a visitor with a camera.

Miranda shrugged. "Average height, average looks. Forties, at a guess. He said he was a birder, and we get a fair number of them. He went out every day with a camera and binoculars. He didn't appear to take any particular interest in Sammy."

Tyler drummed his fingers on the table, mind moving rapidly through possibilities. "When exactly was he here? What do you know about him?"

"Last month some time." She frowned. "He stayed about a week, I think. When we get home, I can look him up on the computer and be more exact."

She met Tyler's gaze, hers perplexed. "Why? Why would he take the picture and send it to you?"

"I don't know. But I think the sooner we find out, the better." He shoved back his chair and glanced at his watch. "Do you think another hour of this will satisfy Sammy?"

Miranda's smile erased some of the worry in her face. "Nothing short of finding the dolphin will satisfy Sammy, but I think he'll have to be content with that today."

"I'll go help him look." A very good idea, he told himself as he walked away from Miranda. Because the longer he stayed in the same room with her, the more he wanted to kiss her again.

He found Sammy burrowing into the depths of a large closet off the game room and set to work to move some of the folding tables and chairs that were stowed there. Unfortunately that didn't serve as enough of a distraction.

What had he been thinking, to let himself get that close to Miranda? He must have been crazy. One moment he'd been noticing how the sunlight through the window brought out the gold flecks in her eyes, and the next he'd been holding her.

He'd known it was a mistake while he was doing it, but he couldn't stop himself. Kissing Miranda again had felt like water after thirst or food after hunger—something so elemental it couldn't be denied. It had felt like coming home after years of wandering.

But it wasn't, and they both knew it. Whatever the source of that lightning between them, it didn't translate into marriage. They'd tried that, and they'd both come away scarred.

Now there was Sammy to figure into the mix, making it even more difficult. They couldn't risk letting Sammy be hurt by their impossible attraction.

*Don't count on anyone. They'll only let you down.*

His father's words didn't quite fit in this situation. He and Miranda had let each other down.

Sammy sat on his heels and stared disconsolately into the empty closet. "Do you think maybe there's a secret hiding place?"

Tyler reached in to thump the walls with his fist. "Seems pretty solid to me. I'm sorry, son."

It was the first time he'd used the word to Sammy. He held his breath, waiting for a reaction.

But Sammy's mind seemed to be on the failure of his search, not on anything his father might say. "I thought it would be here." He straightened, seizing a stack of games to put back. "But I'm not giving up. I'm going to find it."

Had his son's stubbornness come from him or Miranda? They probably both had more than their fair share.

"Maybe we can look some more another time. I think your mother wants to start back soon."

He thought the boy would argue, but Sammy seemed to realize it would do no good. "We can come again some other day, okay?"

"Okay." Tyler hefted one of the folding tables. "Let's get these things put away."

Doing a simple job with his son was oddly satisfying. Had he and his father ever done anything so mundane together? Not that he could recall. His father had always been too busy with the company. Their rare times together had been scripted—business social events where he was supposed to occupy some colleague's children while his father closed a deal.

"I want to bring that box of cars down, then I'm ready." Sammy darted off.

Tyler went to the living room, but their snack had been cleared away and Miranda was nowhere in sight. He pushed through the front screen door and saw her.

She sat on a fallen log under the palmettos, perfectly still. A few feet from her, a deer nosed its way through the undergrowth.

He eased the door closed. If Miranda knew he was there, she gave no sign. Her entire being was concentrated on the graceful brown creature that moved closer and closer to her.

His throat tightened. Miranda fit into island life as surely as the deer in the woods or the dolphins at play in the sound. She moved to the rhythm of the tides and the seasons.

Little wonder she hadn't been able to adapt to the kind of life he offered her. He'd told himself at the time she hadn't tried, but that had been unfair. She couldn't. She belonged here.

Their son would have to bridge two worlds. That would be difficult enough, without adding uncertainty over the relationship between his mother and father.

Tyler and Miranda would have to step as carefully as the deer did. And no matter how hard they tried, there were no guarantees they could do this without damaging their son.

\* \* \*

"What are you doing?"

The voice startled Miranda, and she inadvertently closed the file she'd been searching. She glanced up.

Tyler stood in the office doorway. The pool of light from her desk lamp didn't quite reach him, making him a dark silhouette against the hallway beyond.

"Looking for the records on our Mr. Dawson." She rolled her chair back from the desk. "I haven't been able to get him off my mind since Sammy told us about him this afternoon, but this is the first chance I've had to look through the records."

Family had surrounded them since they'd returned from Angel Isle. That should have made it easier for her to be near Tyler, but it hadn't. She'd been too aware of the necessity to hide her feelings both from him and from the family.

She'd asked her mother about Dawson, evading explanations for her interest. She hadn't wanted the outpouring of advice that story would have triggered. All in all, she'd been happy to escape into the office once Sammy was in bed.

Tyler crossed the small office and leaned his hip against the desk. He still wore the khakis and dress shirt he'd donned for supper—apparently he wasn't convinced he could appear at the table in jeans.

He glanced at the monthly charts posted along one wall, the filing cabinets, the fax and copy machines. "This isn't what I expected."

"The office? Did you think we did it all with quill pens?"

"Not quite that." He smiled, and she appreciated

the width of the desk between them. She needed something to safeguard her from the effect of that smile. "But the registration desk with the old-fashioned register sends a different message from this."

"People want old-fashioned, down-home charm when they come here. They don't need to know that all the records move from the register straight to my computer."

"Very nice. You probably even have a Web site."

"Thanks to Chloe. She set it up for us." She swiveled to face the computer. "I ought to be able to track everything we have about Dawson—his reservation, how he paid, credit card."

"Ought to be?" His voice came from directly behind her. He'd rounded the desk while she'd focused on the screen, and he stood close to her chair. She felt his hands brush her shoulders, then grip the chair back.

Breathe, she ordered herself. Concentrate. She couldn't let Tyler guess his nearness reminded her vividly of that moment when they'd kissed. He'd obviously been able to dismiss it from his mind. So should she.

Her throat felt tight, and she swallowed. "The trouble is, he didn't make a reservation." She pulled up the relevant screen. Tyler leaned over her shoulder to look at it, and she had to remind herself to breathe again.

"He just walked in?" His question was sharp, and he wore the expression she'd always thought of as his business look—intent, determined, focused.

"Well, it was February. We weren't exactly busy."
She frowned. "It's a little unusual that he didn't even
call to ask if we had a room, but it does happen."

"What about his credit card?"

She clicked to the payment file, then shook her
head. "He paid in cash."

Tyler's hand came down on her shoulder. "You're
not going to tell me that's routine."

"No." She tried to ignore the warmth that trickled
through her at his touch. "No, that's not routine. Most
people use credit cards, a few pay by check. Cash
is—strange."

"I'm beginning to find the mysterious Mr. Dawson
a little too strange to believe." Tyler sounded grim.
"Can you trace his address?"

"Let's have a look." She tried to manage a smile.
"Theo showed me a Web site where you can check
an address anywhere in the country. I don't think I
want to know why teenagers know something like
that."

"Power," he suggested.

"I suppose so." She clicked to the site, trying to
ignore the pressure of Tyler's hand, the feel of his
breath against her cheek as he leaned over. "Let's see
if Alfred Dawson really is at 4423 Steeple Drive in
Detroit."

The answer popped up in seconds, and Tyler saw
it as quickly as she did.

"A phony address." His anger was communicated
through his touch.

"It might not mean anything." She tried to come
up with a logical reason and failed.

"Somehow I can't buy that."

"I guess I can't, either. I asked my mother what she remembered about him."

Tyler turned her swivel chair so she faced him. "And?"

"He didn't make much impression on her, either. But she was surprised when I said he was from Detroit."

"Why?" Tyler's habit of firing one-word questions was unnerving.

"She said she talked to him about things to see in the area, and Charleston was mentioned. He referred to it as the holy city. Nobody does that except died-in-the-wool Charlestonians."

That brought some reaction to his stern expression, so quick she couldn't quite decipher it.

"What is it?" Apprehension colored her voice.

"Winchester Industries has a branch office in Charleston."

"That could just be coincidence."

"That's a few too many coincidences for my peace of mind. Maybe you can believe in this random visitor with the vanishing past who just happens to take a photo of Sammy that just happens to get sent to me, but I can't."

She battled a rush of fear. "If you weren't who you are—"

Tyler's face was set. "If I weren't Tyler Winchester, this wouldn't have happened, is that what you mean?"

"Well, would it?" She tried to push her chair away from him, but he gripped it firmly.

"You knew who I was when you married me."

Her brief flare of anger was extinguished by his tone. "Yes. I knew." She had to deal with the repercussions of that.

He straightened. "I'm going to the office in Charleston tomorrow. I'll find an investigations agency while I'm there and put them onto it. Give me everything you have on Dawson."

Her life was spinning out of control. "I'll get it ready for you."

"Good." He turned away, his mind obviously racing ahead to the next day.

"Tyler, don't forget about the T-ball practice. You promised Sammy you'd be there."

"I'll be back in plenty of time." He focused on her, his expression softening. "Don't worry so much." He touched her cheek lightly. "I'll get to the bottom of this, whatever it is. I'm not going to let anything hurt Sammy."

She nodded, pinning a smile on her face. All Tyler's concern was for their son, and that was the way it should be. Still, she couldn't quite suppress the rebellious little corner of her heart that wished some of his concern were for her.

# Chapter Eight

"He's not coming." Sammy's lower lip came out, and Miranda suspected he was pouting to keep himself from crying.

Miranda glanced at her watch again, then down the street toward the center of the village. Tyler had promised to be back from Charleston in time for Sammy's T-ball practice. He wasn't.

"Come on, Momma." Sammy yanked the car door open and tossed Theo's old ball glove onto the seat. "We'll be late if we don't go now."

She felt like pouting herself. Or crying. Seeing Sammy's hurt was worse than her own. She slid into the car.

"Maybe he got stuck in traffic getting out of Charleston." She'd suggest anything that might wipe the pain from her son's face.

"He could've been here if he wanted to." Sammy clutched the glove, not looking at her as she pulled onto the street. "I knew he wouldn't come."

"Son, maybe you ought to wait and see what your father says before you decide that."

Sammy didn't answer. How could she blame him for his anger and disappointment when she was seething with it, too? This was just what she'd feared would happen when she let Tyler into their lives.

You couldn't keep him out, her conscience reminded her. Once he knew about Sammy, that option wasn't open.

Her eyes searched the bridge to the mainland as they passed it, looking without success for Tyler's burgundy rental car. We agreed we weren't going to let Sammy be hurt. How could you let him down this way?

There was little point in addressing the question to someone who wasn't there. But when Tyler arrived, he'd have to answer her.

Something prickled in her mind, refusing to go away until she looked at it.

You never confronted Tyler about anything when you were married.

She looked at the truth with dismay. Had she really been that young, that much in awe of him? Had she been that much of a doormat?

She drew up under the live oaks that ringed the practice field, clenching the steering wheel for a moment of prayer as Sammy darted from the car.

*Lord, I'm angry right now with Tyler. I don't want to confront him out of my own hurt. Help me to make him understand his responsibility to his son.*

She wouldn't let her feelings get in the way. She

wouldn't repeat the pattern she'd begun when they were married. This time Tyler would be called to account.

Practice was long over when the moment came to put her resolution into action. Miranda sat alone on the front porch when Tyler's car finally pulled into the driveway after supper. The family was tactfully avoiding the area to give her free rein with Tyler. She would need it.

He mounted the porch steps, then put his briefcase down. The suit jacket he'd worn when he left was slung over his shoulder, but he still looked business-like and intimidating in the dress shirt and striped tie that announced his status.

"Waiting for me?"

"Yes." He obviously didn't remember. Anger for her child burned along her veins. How long would it take him to realize what he'd done? "We have to talk."

He nodded, leaning against the railing. "Dan Carpenter, who's in charge of the Charleston office, was able to recommend a private investigations agency. I talked with them, gave them all the information we had. They hope to get a line on our Mr. Dawson before long."

If he expected congratulations on that, he was doomed to disappointment. "And did some disaster hit the company this afternoon?"

He frowned. "No, of course not. Why?"

She shoved herself out of the rocking chair, letting it creak back and forth. "Why? Because I couldn't imagine that anything less would keep you from fulfilling your promise to your son.'' She planted her fists on her hips. ''You don't even remember, do you?''

She watched him thinking it over, mentally checking his calendar. She saw the moment when it registered.

''T-ball practice.''

''You told Sammy you'd be there.''

Annoyance flared in his eyes at her tone, and he crossed his arms over his chest. ''I had business to take care of.'' He was clearly not used to accounting for himself to anyone.

''More important business than keeping your promise?''

''Look, I forgot.'' His belligerent attitude eased, and he put his hands against the railing on either side of him. ''I'm sorry. Was he upset?''

The sign of concern for Sammy heartened her. ''Yes.'' She wouldn't pretend this wasn't important, because it was. ''He was upset. He said he knew you wouldn't come.''

Tyler winced at that. ''What did you tell him?''

''I said he should wait and talk to you before he decided that. That maybe you had a good reason.''

''I take it business isn't a good enough reason.''

*Please, Lord, help me make him see.*

''Not for breaking a promise.''

''Come on, Miranda. People break promises all the time.''

Maybe the people in your life do, Tyler. Not the people in mine.

"A promise between parent and child is…well, it's sacred. You can't treat it lightly."

He frowned. "You make it sound like an article of faith."

"It is." She took a breath, searching for the words that would make him understand. "I can't separate faith out from parenting. I know I can't be as good a parent as God is, but I have to try."

Pain flickered in his eyes. "If I compared God to my father—" He stopped, shook his head. "Okay, I was wrong not to keep my promise. I don't have a good excuse. I'm still trying to figure out this parenting stuff."

Meaning it was her fault he didn't have much experience as a father. They'd never get past that.

"I know." She forced her voice to be steady. "This is one of those situations where you learn from your mistakes. But this one really hurt him."

His mouth tightened. "Where is Sammy? I owe him an apology."

"He's down at the dock. I'll go with you."

He lifted his eyebrows as they started down the steps. "Afraid I'll make a mess of it on my own?"

"Not if you're honest with him." How much should she push him? "Try to open up to him, Tyler. That's what he needs."

For a moment she thought he wouldn't reply. There was no sound but the crunch of their footsteps on the shell-covered path and the distant cry of a gull. Sammy's small figure perched on the end of the dock, the channel beyond him turning purple in the setting sun.

"There's not much call for opening up in my life," Tyler said finally. His gaze was fixed on Sammy. "I'm probably not good at it. But I'll try."

*Please, Lord,* she prayed as they reached the dock. *Please let them hear each other.*

Tyler's movements were slow as they approached their son, as if Sammy were a wild creature, not to be startled. "Hi, Sammy." He squatted next to him.

Sammy pulled his knees up and wrapped his arms around them. "Hey," he mumbled.

"Okay if we sit down?"

He got a shrug of the shoulders in answer but seemed to take that for a yes. He sat on the dock next to Sammy, not quite close enough to touch.

*Please, Lord.* Miranda sat, folding her legs. *I'm not even sure where Tyler stands in relation to You now. I don't know if he's asking for Your help. But I'm asking. Please help him.*

"I'm sorry I missed your practice today."

Another shrug. "It's okay."

But it wasn't. Her heart hurt for him.

"I wanted to be there."

Sammy looked at him, his small face set. For a moment she saw the resemblance between them so clearly that she could hardly bear it.

"If you wanted to, you would have."

The logic of a seven-year-old was direct. To do him justice, Tyler didn't try to argue with it.

"I guess you've got a point there. I didn't set out to miss it, but I got busy talking to someone, and I forgot."

Open up to him, Tyler. She thought the words so strongly she almost felt he could hear them.

Tyler leaned forward, his elbows on his knees. She spared a brief thought for what the rough planks were probably doing to his dress trousers. He didn't seem to care.

"You know, Sammy, I guess I haven't quite figured out this father stuff yet. But I remember…"

He paused, glanced at her. She nodded, trying to look encouraging. He couldn't give up now, even though Sammy wasn't responding.

"I was probably a little older than you are. My school had this program where kids' parents came in and talked about their careers."

"Career day," Sammy muttered without raising his head. "We have that, too."

"I was at a boarding school, where you actually live at school. My father said he'd come for career day. It was the first time he'd ever promised something like that. He'd always been too busy before."

Tyler seemed to look into the past, to the boy he'd been. "I was really excited. I told all my friends he was coming. I remember the teacher even had me make a name sign for him."

The timbre of Tyler's voice had deepened. She heard it and knew she was hearing genuine emotion.

Sammy seemed to recognize it, too. He looked up, fixing his gaze on his father's face. "What happened?"

Tyler shrugged. "He didn't show up. The other parents came, and they sat at a long table with their name signs in front of them. I sat there the whole period and looked at my father's sign and his empty chair.''

"You felt bad." Sammy's loving heart filled his voice.

"Yes."

She didn't think Tyler would say anything more. Then he cleared his throat.

"He hadn't forgotten. Something else just came up that he thought was more important. He never even said he was sorry."

His words pressed on her heart. She knew what Sammy didn't—that the story he'd told wasn't just an isolated incident. Tyler's father had never been there for his son.

Why hadn't she realized the effect of that on Tyler when they were married? Guilt swept over her.

No wonder it had been so important to him to take over after his father's heart attack. He'd still been trying to prove himself, and she hadn't understood that.

Did that lonely little boy still lurk inside Tyler? He'd built his life around not being emotionally involved with anyone, but maybe he needed family more than he thought he did.

"Sammy, I want to do better than my father did. I'm sorry I let you down. I hope you can forgive me."

Sammy's eyes were suspiciously bright with tears, but he wouldn't let them fall. He nodded, then stuck out his hand. They shook hands solemnly.

Her eyes were wet. Miranda blinked rapidly, trying not to make a fool of herself. Neither of them would thank her for crying over them. Seeing the two of them bond with each other wrenched her heart. This was the way it should have been from the beginning. Maybe it would have been, if she'd only had the courage to try harder.

Tyler hadn't felt this much relief when a risky business gamble had paid off. He smiled at his son, hoping he wasn't going to disgrace himself by tearing up. He wanted Sammy to like him, not to feel pity for him.

"Thank you, Sammy." The feel of his son's small hand in his gave him a visceral surge of totally unexpected love, knocking him completely off balance.

Of course he'd thought he'd love his son. He'd assumed it would come slowly, growing as they got to know each other.

He hadn't anticipated this overwhelming emotion, sweeping everything else aside with its power, so strong he didn't know what to do with it. Wherever this relationship was taking him, there was no turning back.

He put his hand lightly on Sammy's shoulder, afraid to give in to the longing to hug him. "You're a better person than I was. I guess we have to thank your mother for that."

He looked at Miranda. She leaned against the rough wooden post, her gray sweatshirt blending into it. The setting sun made her hair blaze like a flame, and her green eyes sparkled with unshed tears.

"Sammy's a good kid. I've had good stuff to work with." Her voice trembled just a little, and he knew she didn't want their son to hear that tremor.

His hand still rested on their son's shoulder, and he didn't want to let go. "What do you say, Sammy? You think I could make another try at going to T-ball practice with you?"

Sammy nodded. "Next practice is Thursday after school. Okay?"

"Sounds great. I'll be there, no matter what. I promise."

"Speaking of school…" Miranda sounded as if she had herself under control.

Sammy's nose wrinkled. "It can't be my bedtime already."

"It will be by the time you have your bath and your story. You scoot on up to the house, sugar. We'll be up in a few minutes."

The boy scrambled to his feet. "Okay, Momma." He turned toward Tyler. "Good night…Daddy."

Before Tyler could respond, he darted off, running full tilt toward the house.

He'd had the wind knocked out of him. "He called me Daddy."

"Yes, he did." Her smile shimmered on the edge of tears.

"That's a pretty decent reward for forgetting my promise."

"It wasn't for forgetting. Or even for apologizing. It was because you shared yourself with him."

He hadn't heard that gentle, loving note in Miranda's voice directed at him in a long time. It rocked him nearly as much as hearing Sammy call him Daddy, and it made him grope for something solid to hang on to.

Indian River Area Library
3546 S. Straits Hwy.
P.O. Box 160

"Believe me, it wasn't hard to come up with a time when my father let me down. They were too numerous to count."

"I'm sorry. I wish..."

"What do you wish, Miranda?"

He moved next to her, watching the way the light touched her skin with gold. On the waterway a boat arrowed toward the distant shore, darkening as the sun slipped lower. They were alone.

"I wish I'd understood, back then, about your relationship with your father. I could have done better if I had."

Regret and guilt showed on her expressive face—regret for the girl she'd been, guilt over whatever she imagined she could have done differently.

"It wasn't your fault." He tried to look at their marriage without the anger that had consumed him since he'd learned about her deception. "We were both too young to know what we were doing."

"We thought we did."

"You think you know everything at eighteen and twenty. It takes a few years to realize how wrong you are." Impelled by something he wasn't sure he understood, he smoothed a strand of auburn hair from her face, letting his fingertips linger against the smooth curve of her cheek.

Her gaze met his, startled and aware. Her lips softened, parting a little on a sigh that seemed to echo the soft shush of waves against the dock.

That sound had accompanied their first kiss. They'd walked barefoot along the beach in the afterglow of sunset, letting the warm waves wash over their feet.

He'd stopped, turned her toward him and kissed her, sensing nothing was going to be the same again.

That was then, and this was now. Eight years later, and apparently not any wiser.

"Tyler." She said his name softly, so softly he seemed to sense it instead of hear it.

His hand moved of its own volition, cradling her cheek, tilting her face to his. Slowly he covered her lips with his.

She was soft, so soft. She turned more fully toward him, and his arms slid around her, holding her as closely as his lips held hers. A wave of longing and tenderness swept over him, strong enough to pull him under.

His heart beat in time with the waves, as if his blood moved to some eternal rhythm he hadn't ever been aware of. His lips moved to her temple. He felt the pulse that beat there, and it, like the waves, seemed to move in time with his.

Miranda settled against him as if she'd come home. Or maybe as if they'd never been apart.

"Tyler." She whispered his name against his chest.

Something swelled inside his heart, longing to break free. Emotions he'd denied for years beat against his control.

It's not safe, he warned himself. It's not wise. Don't get involved.

Don't count on anyone else. They'll only let you down.

Sluggishly, as if he moved through water, he drew away from her. He watched the light in Miranda's eyes die.

He couldn't do this. Not because of what his father had believed, but because of what he suddenly saw so clearly about himself.

This wasn't about anyone else letting him down. It was about him letting them down.

He'd have to struggle to be the man his son needed. It would be downright impossible to be the man Miranda needed.

# Chapter Nine

Miranda pressed the rolling pin firmly, spreading the piecrust dough in a circle on the floured board. She found comfort in the familiar, soothing movements. Doing something routine was a relief from the tensions of the past week.

This old kitchen was equally comforting. At five or six she'd knelt on a stool at the counter, painstakingly rolling out the scraps of dough her mother had given her, trying to be just like Momma. Later, she and Chloe and the twins had sat at the scrubbed pine table in the evenings, doing homework while Momma and Daddy talked over the day's doings in soft, contented voices.

She looked at the large calendar posted on the kitchen wall. Crowded with notations, it kept track of who was where in the busy Caldwell clan. Today, Saturday, it showed that Tyler and Sammy were at T-ball practice. It also showed her that one week was gone from Tyler's month.

A burst of panic touched her—one week down, three to go. Tyler probably checked the days off in his engagement book or his electronic organizer, counting down the moments until he could leave Caldwell Cove and get back to his real life.

The life that had no place in it for her. She'd known that for years and had it reinforced since the night on the dock when he'd kissed her. His immediate withdrawal and the efforts he'd made in the days since to avoid her had shown how much he regretted that act.

He'd left for Charleston each day immediately after having breakfast with Sammy, returning scrupulously by the time Sammy got home from school. He'd been pleasant, polite and cooperative. He'd felt as distant from her as if he were already in Baltimore, living the life that didn't include her.

She fit the crust into the pie pan, fluting the edge with the quick twist of the fingers her mother had taught her when she'd been deemed old enough to start baking real pies instead of playing with the dough. Comforting or not, making pies for Sunday dinner wasn't enough to distract her mind from the treadmill it had walked since that night on the dock.

Tyler didn't want anything from her except cooperation in their joint parenting. His kisses had been a fluke, perhaps a reaction to some faded memory of the people they'd once been. He must have been horrified at the mistake he'd almost repeated.

Unfortunately those moments had shown her the truth she could no longer avoid. She still loved Tyler. She'd buried those feelings in family and work and her son, but a few kisses and a moment in his arms had brought the flame blazing to life.

At some level, she'd known that would be inevitable from the moment she'd walked into the hall and seen him. She pressed a floury hand against the front of her T-shirt, as if that would ease the hurt. Her relationship with Tyler was beyond repair. All she could do was concentrate on making the changes in Sammy's life as smooth and easy as possible for all three of them.

The screen door slammed, and Sammy raced into the kitchen. He sported a streak of dirt on one cheek, and his T-shirt looked as if he'd rolled around in the grass, but he was smiling.

"Hey, Momma. I smell pies. Did you make some cinnamon crust for me?"

"What's cinnamon crust?" Tyler stopped inside the door.

Miranda swallowed, her mouth suddenly dry. It ought to be illegal for a man to look that good in jeans and a T-shirt.

"Leftover pieces of piecrust. We always bake them with cinnamon sugar for hungry little boys." She held the baking sheet out to Sammy, who grabbed one. "And big boys." She offered them to Tyler.

He dropped the ball glove he carried onto the kitchen table, broke off a piece and popped it into his mouth. His eyes widened.

"Wonderful. Why haven't America's baking companies started putting these on the supermarket shelves?"

Tyler would be easier to ignore if he weren't there,

filling up her kitchen, an errant crumb clinging to his lips.

"Because they're only good if they're homemade crusts, fresh from the oven. One of those things that can't be mass produced."

Would there be homemade goodies in Sammy's life when he went to visit his father in Baltimore?

Three weeks, a little voice in her head reminded her. Only three weeks, and then you'll have to make plans for your son to spend some of his days far away, living a life you can barely imagine.

Sammy grabbed another crust. "I'm going to find Granddaddy and tell him about practice." He got to the door, then glanced at Tyler. "Thanks, Daddy."

Then he was gone, and she was right where she didn't want to be—alone with Tyler.

"He enjoys saying that, you know." She picked up the bowl of apple slices and started filling crusts.

"I have to say it feels pretty good to me, too." He leaned against the counter, keeping a careful foot of space between them.

"You don't look very glad. What's wrong?" It was scary how well she could still read his expression after all this time. Something had put that brooding look in his dark eyes.

He shrugged, pointing toward the glove on the table. "I bought a new baseball glove for Sammy, gave it to him when we went to practice. He didn't want it."

She pressed her hands against the counter, not sure what to say. If only he'd asked her first, she might have foreseen the difficulty. "I hope he was polite."

"Oh, very polite." His eyes were stormy. "But very definite. He'd rather use his old one."

She heard the hurt under the annoyance in his voice. This was the first gift he'd given his son, and Sammy hadn't wanted it.

She had to try to make this right, if she could. "Did he tell you why?"

"No." He frowned at her. "What do you know about it?"

She wiped her hands on a tea towel, then turned to face him. "I'm sure he appreciated your thoughtfulness. It's just that the one he's been using was Theo's. And before that either David or Daniel's."

She smiled, remembering the squabble between her brothers. "One of them lost his, and they both claim the remaining glove is his."

"So Sammy would rather have an old glove because it belonged to Theo." He obviously didn't care which twin had lost his glove. He only cared that Sammy had rejected his gift.

"It's kind of a tradition. Your younger brother would feel that way about something you passed on to him."

Or didn't people like the Winchesters pass things on from one child to the next? Maybe she was making this worse by bringing up his family.

"I doubt it. My brother and I aren't very close. And knowing Josh, I'm sure he'd prefer something new to something I'd already used."

She was probably getting in deeper, but she had to contest that.

"Younger brothers always look up to older ones.

Josh probably feels that way about you, even if he's never said it. He followed your footsteps into the company, didn't he?''

''I suspect that had more to do with getting a large salary for doing very little than from any idea of being like me.'' He shook his head, an errant lock of dark hair tumbling onto his forehead. ''Why are we talking about my brother, anyway?''

Did he really not understand?

''Because he is your brother. Sammy's uncle.''

Tyler folded his arms across his chest. ''Don't go running away with the idea that Josh will be the kind of uncle your brothers have been. He wouldn't know how.''

''Sammy will see him when he comes to visit you, won't he?'' She tried to make that eventuality sound as routine and everyday as a trip to the grocery.

''I suppose so.'' He searched her face. ''Are you worrying about that?''

''Not about your brother, no. But about what Sammy's life will be like.'' A lump constricted her throat. ''When he's away from here.''

''I'll take good care of him.'' His voice softened. He reached toward her, almost but not quite touching. ''You must know that.''

''I know.'' Somehow that wasn't as reassuring as it should be, not when she tried to imagine those spaces in her son's life that wouldn't include her. ''What about church?''

''What about it?'' The softness disappeared.

She lifted her chin. This was one thing she'd go toe-to-toe over if necessary. ''Church is an important part of Sammy's life. I want your assurance that won't change when he's with you.''

''I'll see that he goes,'' he said shortly.

''With you.'' She pressed the point. ''You can't just drop him off as if he has to go but other things are more important to you.''

A muscle twitched in his jaw. ''Sounds as if you're making all the decisions about Sammy and expecting me to go along with them.''

''About this I am.'' Standing fast in the face of Tyler's irritation wasn't as difficult as she'd expected. Maybe she'd grown up a bit.

''Fine. I promise I'll go to church with him when he stays with me.'' He stalked to the door, annoyance filling his voice and his movements. ''Now if you'll excuse me, I have work to do.''

An annoyed Tyler wasn't as much of a threat to her vulnerable heart as he was when he said her name in that soft, masculine rumble. Maybe, if she could annoy him enough, she could learn to harden her heart against him. But that didn't seem very likely.

If his church in Baltimore was like this one, he might be less reluctant to attend. Tyler leaned against a pew back the next morning, waiting for Miranda to finish talking with all the people who had something to say to her after the worship service.

What was it that felt so different about the Caldwell Cove church? He glanced around the sanctuary, small enough to fit four or five of them into the vast nave of the church he normally attended a few times a year.

This simple, whitewashed structure boasted plain

oak pews and a slightly faded carpet runner down the center aisle. The sanctuary's only claim to elegance was the ancient stained-glass windows that glowed in the spring sunlight.

An old-fashioned church, it had an old-fashioned charm. The minister had been neither profound nor philosophical, but the love he projected to his parishioners glowed as much as the windows did. The warmth filling the small sanctuary had nothing to do with the temperature.

He didn't have to continue attending the same church in Baltimore just because his parents had been long-time members. He could find someplace else to go when Sammy stayed with him. Miranda had certainly made it clear that going to church wasn't negotiable.

Across the length of the pew, Miranda continued to talk, apparently in no hurry. She tilted her head in response to some comment, her hair brushing the shoulders of the cream dress she wore. Her profile was serene and lovely.

Beautiful, in fact. He suspected the simple dress was several years out of date, and no professional stylist had touched her hair, but Miranda didn't need polishing to shine. Her light came from within.

Uncomfortable at the direction his thoughts had taken, he moved to the dolphin window.

"Pretty thing, isn't it?" Miranda's grandmother came toward him, nodding at the window.

"It's lovely." He tensed, half expecting her to take him to task for his presence on the island. Everyone knew Gran Caldwell was the matriarch of the clan. He was surprised she hadn't tackled him before this.

The elderly woman didn't seem to have battle in mind as she stared at the dolphin. Whatever she felt, no emotion showed. The clean, strong lines of her face had elegance, too, like the windows. She was what Miranda would be in fifty or sixty years.

"My grandson Adam's fiancée did that window. I reckon you heard that."

"Miranda told me."

"Told you the story of the first dolphin, too, I suppose." She nodded toward the bracket behind the pulpit where the wooden dolphin had once stood.

"Yes. Well, Sammy told me most of it. He wrote a story about it for school."

He thought of what Miranda had said—that her father and his brother had been at odds for years after the incident with the dolphin and her father's injury. That must have been hard on their mother.

"Should have the dolphin here for weddings, at least." She continued to stare at the shelf, filled with flowers.

"Why weddings?"

She switched her gaze to him, and he had the odd sensation that those wise old eyes saw right through him. "Thought you said you'd heard the story."

"Maybe Sammy left something out. I don't remember anything about weddings."

She shook her head. "That boy's at the stage where he thinks love and such is foolishness. That's probably why he didn't say anything. The first Caldwell carved the dolphin out of love for his bride. Folks always believed it brought special blessings on those who wed under its gaze.''

An uneasy feeling prickled along the back of his neck. Special blessings? He and Miranda hadn't married under the eyes of the dolphin, and the only blessing that had come of their marriage was Sammy.

''Hasn't been right, having Caldwells marry without it,'' she said firmly, as if he'd argued.

''No, I guess not.'' Was she thinking of him and Miranda, their marriage broken before it began?

His uneasiness intensified. Was that what lay behind Sammy's determination to find the dolphin? Could he possibly imagine that restoring it would bring his parents together?

If Sammy thought that, he was setting himself up for disappointment. Tyler tried to tell himself the idea was nonsense, but the uneasiness clung like a burr.

''Reckon I'll see you over to Jeff's for dinner.'' Miranda's grandmother didn't offer to shake hands. ''I'd best get my salad ready to go.'' With another glance toward the dolphin shelf, she made her way toward the door.

Trying to shake oppressive thoughts about the dolphin and Sammy from his mind, Tyler moved along the pew toward Miranda, who was concluding her conversation.

She gave him a quick smile. If appearing in church with him had bothered her, she wasn't letting it show.

''I guess we'd better get along over to Uncle Jeff's place.'' She started toward the door, and he followed. ''You'll get to take on the whole Caldwell clan at once.''

"Is this get-together for my benefit? Are they preparing tar and feathers?"

A smile tugged at her lips as she stepped into a shaft of sunlight. "Not that I know of, though I wouldn't put anything past those brothers of mine. No, we just all have Sunday dinner together at least once a month."

"Another tradition." To his surprise, the words came out sounding wistful. There'd been precious little tradition in his family, unless the predictable fact that his father would miss every celebration counted as one.

Miranda didn't seem to notice. She was glancing around the church lawn, apparently counting heads.

People still stood in small clusters, probably catching up on the events of the past week. Some of the children had started a game of tag under the swaying Spanish moss of the live oaks. The girls' pale dresses fluttered around their legs. Across the narrow street, a boat revved its motor at the dock—some Sunday sailor off for a ride, probably. What did a scene like this have to do with him?

"We'd best collect Sammy and get on our way," Miranda said.

"Just a moment." He stopped her with a hand on her arm.

She glanced up at his touch, something unguarded showing in her eyes for an instant. "What's wrong? If you don't want to go—"

"Of course I intend to go," he said impatiently. "I told Sammy I would. But there's something I need to talk with you about first."

He'd better tell Miranda what he feared was behind Sammy's search for the dolphin. Probably she'd laugh at the idea, and then he'd be able to forget it.

"What is it?" Apprehension colored her voice, as if she felt anything he wanted to discuss must be unpleasant.

"Your grandmother told me the rest of the story about the dolphin." An elderly couple moved slowly past them. He stepped off the walk and lowered his voice. "The part you left out. About how couples who marry under the dolphin's gaze are supposed to be especially blessed."

"That's how the story goes." Her cheeks grew pink. She was probably thinking, as he had, that there hadn't been anything particularly blessed about the painful brevity of their marriage.

"It made me wonder if that's what's behind this treasure hunt of Sammy's." He couldn't think of any tactful way of saying this. "Do you think he's got some notion that finding the dolphin is going to fix his parents' marriage?"

The words sounded even more foolish said out loud than in his mind. He waited for Miranda to tell him how ridiculous that was.

Instead, dismay filled her face. "It never occurred to me. If that's what he's thinking, we've got to do something about it."

"You know him better than I do." For the first time, he didn't feel resentful at the thought. "If it never occurred to you, it probably didn't to him."

Worry lines crinkled her forehead. "He has been awfully obsessed with that story lately. I wish I could say the idea is impossible, but I can't." She met his gaze, her green eyes clouded. "Tyler, what are we going to do?"

We, she'd said. For the first time, she'd included him in a decision.

"We can't do anything right now." Sammy, abandoning his game, was running toward them. At the curb, Caldwells piled into various vehicles. "We've got Sunday dinner to attend. Let's give it some time. Maybe I'm wrong."

Sammy ran up and grabbed his hand, and it seemed natural to take Miranda's arm. Linked, they started down the walk. They might almost look like a family.

Miranda balanced the pie carrier with the apple crumb pies as she crossed the veranda of Twin Oaks, Uncle Jefferson's house. Tyler came behind her, carrying two lemon meringues. If he felt any nervousness about encountering the entire Caldwell clan, he didn't show it. His face was perfectly composed.

They went through the open front door and into the spacious center hallway. She glanced at the graceful sweep of the curving staircase, the crystal chandelier, the rice-carved drop-leaf table surmounted by its Empire mirror, trying to see them through Tyler's eyes.

He lifted an eyebrow at her. "I take it this is the wealthy branch of the family."

"You might say that." Everyone knew Uncle Jeff put success ahead of everything else. He and Tyler might have a lot in common.

Except that Uncle Jeff had begun to change in the

last year, seeming to want to make amends for the long breach between him and her father. She couldn't think of anything that was likely to make Tyler change.

She swept that unproductive thought from her mind. "We'll put the pies on the buffet."

He followed her into the dining room—more crystal, more rice-carved mahogany. The room's French doors stood open to the veranda overlooking the marsh. Most folks were gathered out there, except for a cluster of kids checking out the bounty on the long table.

"You young 'uns get out of my way now, y'heah?" Miz Becky, the Gullah housekeeper who kept Twin Oaks running smoothly, swept through the door from the kitchen with a steaming tureen in her hands.

She caught sight of them as she put the dish of sweet potatoes down, and her face broke into a broad smile. "Miranda, child, it's good to see you. This here must be Sammy's daddy."

Tyler put the pies he carried on the sideboard and shook hands.

"This is Miz Becky. She takes care of everyone at Twin Oaks."

Miranda didn't say what else she was thinking— that Miz Becky was a fount of knowledge where people were concerned. She'd be happy to be on the back porch right now, snapping beans into a bowl with Miz Becky, listening to her wise counsel about the difficult art of raising children.

Tyler nodded toward the laden table. "You must be a gourmet cook, as well, if you produced all that."

"It's nothing. Everybody bring something, it's not too much for anybody." Miz Becky raised her voice. "Jenny, you go on and tell your granddaddy the food is up now. Somebody better ask the blessing 'fore it gets cold."

The group on the veranda must have heard her, because Caldwells started streaming into the dining room. Her cousin Adam held hands with his fiancée, Tory, and the sight touched her heart. For so long it had seemed Adam would never find his true love, but now happiness shone in their faces. In June, dolphin or no, they'd be wed at St. Andrew's.

Should she point out to Sammy the happy marriages that had taken place even without the dolphin? Not until she'd discussed it with Tyler. She glanced at his strong face, familiar yet somehow hiding thoughts and beliefs she knew nothing of.

From now on, she had to take his opinions into account in every decision she made for Sammy. She wasn't a single parent any longer. Tyler had as much to say in raising their son as she did. The idea sent a shiver sliding along her arms.

*I'm not ready.* She sent up an almost involuntary prayer. *I don't want to share, and I don't want Sammy to accept Tyler's values.*

That was at the core of her resistance, she knew suddenly. She'd loved Tyler, married him in spite of common sense. She loved him still, as hopeless as that was.

But that love didn't keep her from looking at Tyler

honestly. Every now and then, she'd get glimpses of the boy she'd fallen for, think she saw the man he could be. Then he'd turn back into Tyler the business tycoon, and she was afraid that could never change.

# Chapter Ten

Tyler snapped the phone shut with a quick movement and slid it into his pocket. He stood on the inn's porch, looking at the fishing boats moving down the channel. Josh's early morning call probably meant nothing at all, but he couldn't shake off the uneasiness that gripped him.

The fact that Josh, of all people, was in the office this early on a Monday morning was startling enough. The fact that Josh was concerned about business was downright astonishing.

Tyler planted his hands on the porch railing, wishing it were the polished surface of his desk. He'd talked with Henry several times over the last few days, and his assistant had assured him all was fine with the Warren deal. Henry had years of experience to back him up. Nevertheless—

In view of Josh's concern it wouldn't be a bad idea to go to the office for a couple of days. Sammy would understand if he explained it to him, wouldn't he?

Miranda was another story. Instinct told him she wouldn't look favorably on his leaving just when Sammy was warming up to him. Still, she'd been the one to mention the possibility that first night, when she'd brought her proposition to him.

That night had been a little over a week ago, but it felt like forever. In such a short time his life had changed beyond recognition. Would he go back, if he could, to a time before the photo of Sammy arrived on his desk?

A cold hand gripped his heart at the thought. If it hadn't been for that mysterious visitor who'd mailed the picture to him, he might never have known he had a son.

Now that he did, his business success had become more meaningful. He had a son to inherit what he'd built, instead of just hordes of eager relatives with their hands out.

He didn't intend to let anything sour this deal. If that meant a few days away from the island, so be it. Miranda would have to understand. He went quickly into the house.

He poked his head into the office, then walked through the dining room and the kitchen. No Miranda, but Sallie was pouring a cup of coffee.

"Miranda?" He raised his eyebrows.

She gestured with her mug toward the back door. "She's out at the shed, working on Mary Lou."

Mary Lou? He pushed through the screen door, then crossed the lawn to the weathered shed that sat on the edge of the marsh.

He paused in the doorway, letting his eyes adjust

to the dim interior. Wearing her usual uniform of jeans and T-shirt, Miranda bent over an elderly bicycle, a can of oil in her hand. She'd tied her hair back with a yellow ribbon, but curls escaped to cluster against her neck.

"Performing surgery on that thing?" The bike in question was an old-fashioned girl's bike with coaster brakes and a wicker basket attached to the handlebars. "It looks terminal."

She looked up at his approach, giving him the smile that had once twisted his heart out of shape. Not any longer, he assured himself.

"How can you talk that way about Mary Lou? She's one of my oldest friends."

"I can believe the old part." He squatted next to her. "Did someone take away your car keys?"

"No." Her heart-shaped face took on a wary look. "Sammy's getting a two-wheeler for his birthday, and I thought I'd get Mary Lou in shape so I can ride with him. Just until I'm sure he knows how to handle himself."

"His birthday." He repeated her words slowly. "When is it?"

"Thursday." Miranda's look turned defensive. "You knew the date. I showed you his birth certificate."

Clearly something he should have remembered. He wasn't very good at this father business. "You might have reminded me."

Miranda stood, dusting off the knees of her jeans. She lifted the bike to spin the front wheel.

"I guess you know now." Her voice was carefully

neutral, as if she was determined not to betray whatever she thought about a father who didn't remember his son's birthday.

He stood, too, frowning. "About this bicycle..."

"I know she doesn't look like much, but she'll do for what I have in mind," Miranda said quickly.

"Not this one, although I think you're wrong about that. The bicycle Sammy is getting for his birthday. You've bought it already?"

"Not exactly." The wariness was back in her eyes. "I ordered it. I have to go pick it up tomorrow."

Resentment pricked him. "You're giving Sammy a new bicycle for his birthday. What do I get to give him that could possibly be more exciting than that?"

She leaned the bike against a workbench. "We're not in a competition, Tyler. Sammy will love whatever you give him."

"I haven't done very well so far." Like the baseball glove, for instance.

She studied him for a moment, as if assessing how much it bothered him. "Well, how about if we go in on the bike together? Trust me, this is a gift he won't turn down. He's been wanting a new bike for ages."

He'd like to find something even bigger than a bicycle, but he recognized how foolish that would be. He and Miranda weren't competing, as she'd said. Little as he knew about parenting, he knew that wouldn't be good for Sammy.

"Okay. The bike is from both of Sammy's parents. Where do we pick it up?"

"You don't have to go with me. I can manage it myself."

That was predictable. "I'm sure you can, but you're not going to."

Her lips twitched. "Has anybody mentioned to you lately how stubborn you are?"

"Seems to me I've heard that a time or two. I don't think I have a monopoly on it."

Her smile took over, making her green eyes sparkle. "You may have a point there. Okay. I ordered it from a bike shop out on the highway near Savannah. They said I could pick it up tomorrow morning."

"We'll pick it up."

He wasn't sure how this had happened. Hadn't he come out here to tell Miranda he had to run up to Baltimore tomorrow? Well, it didn't have to be tomorrow, necessarily.

"By the way, I might need to go to the office for a couple of days soon."

He almost imagined he saw regret in her eyes before her lashes swept down to hide her reaction. "Is that really necessary?"

Was it? He thought again of Josh's call and of Henry's reassurances. "I don't know." The uncharacteristic uncertainty made his voice sharp. "It may be. It was part of our agreement that I'd go back for a few days if I had to, remember?"

"I'm not the one you need to convince. If you're going away, you'd best tell Sammy ahead of time."

Amazing how difficult a simple thing like that sounded. "I thought maybe you'd do that," he said, knowing what her answer would be.

Her smile flickered again. "Sorry. Breaking bad

news is part of being a parent. You may as well start getting into practice.''

Oddly enough, he liked the fact that she expected something of him. ''Meaning I don't get to just do the fun stuff.''

''No way.'' She wiped her hands with a paper towel from the workbench. ''Do you really have to go to Baltimore? Can't you take care of whatever it is from the Charleston office?''

He shook his head. ''It's an entirely different division.''

She looked at him blankly, and he realized he'd never talked to her about the changes that had taken place in the corporation over the past few years.

''Charleston is the home office for a group of textile mills in Georgia and South Carolina. We acquired them a couple of years ago. They fit in well with the rest of our holdings.''

''And this problem doesn't have anything to do with textiles.'' If she wondered why he'd decided to expand into her part of the world, she didn't mention it.

''Right.'' He rubbed the back of his neck, realizing that the familiar tension had taken up residence there since the talk with Josh. He hadn't noticed it had all but disappeared during the past week. ''We have an important meeting coming up soon over a contract to supply compressors for a company that could be a major new customer for us.''

She leaned against the workbench, looking for all the world as if she really was interested. ''Are there problems with it?''

"There shouldn't be." Again that edge of tension pricked him. "The deal was completely in place when I left. Henry—my assistant, Henry Carmichael—should be able to handle everything without a hitch."

"Then why do you feel you need to go back?"

It was a fair question, but he wasn't used to explaining his actions to anyone. Parenthood changed that, too, it seemed.

"I had a call from Josh this morning. For some reason, he's got the wind up. He can't even tell me why. Just a feeling." He shrugged. "Maybe he's belatedly developing a sense of responsibility. He knows how important this is. Without this contract, we could be facing extensive layoffs. Nobody wants that."

"I didn't realize." Miranda's expressive eyes mirrored guilt. "I didn't think about the people who might be affected by what you do."

"It's not something I can ever forget." He shook his head. "I wish—"

"That you were there," she finished for him.

He looked up, startled. "No. Actually, I was wishing I thought I could count on Josh the way you count on your family."

"That's what families are for. Counting on. And driving you crazy, of course."

He liked the way her face softened when she talked about her family. Liked the way the Caldwells trusted each other, relied on each other.

"My father always said you can't count on anyone but yourself," he said abruptly, surprising himself. "That was his philosophy."

She turned her soft look on him. "That doesn't mean it has to be yours."

"No." He looked at that thought in some surprise. "I guess it doesn't."

The unaccustomed understanding seemed to weave strands of connection between them. He thought Miranda's cheeks flushed a little.

"If you feel you have to go, I'm sure Sammy will understand."

Will you, Miranda? This wasn't about Miranda. This was about his commitment to his son.

"I won't miss his birthday." He said the words with a sureness that surprised him.

Priorities. His father had always put business first. That wasn't the kind of father he wanted to be.

Approval shone in her eyes. "I'm glad you feel that way."

"I'll have Henry go over everything again, just to be on the safe side. It'll be all right."

If he did end up explaining to Sammy that he had to go away, he'd make very sure it was necessary.

He smiled wryly. Maybe the secret to this father business was to do the opposite of everything his father had done. That, and make sure what he did earned that soft look of approval from Miranda.

Had she handled that conversation with Tyler about business correctly? Miranda sat in the porch swing that evening, looking across the inland waterway. This situation was so difficult that, at every step, she felt she risked making an irrevocable move.

Tyler would probably have to figure out for himself

where the balance was between business and parenting. No one else could determine that for him.

Her initial reaction, when she'd believed Tyler couldn't hang around long enough to be any kind of a father, had certainly been easier to live with. But each day, Tyler continued to prove her wrong.

*Lord, I confess I never really thought about the people who depend upon Tyler's business. I've been so focused on the personal that I never looked beyond that. Forgive me for being so shortsighted.*

A few feet away from her, Tyler and her father sat in matching rocking chairs, talking a little, then falling silent, then talking again. Their conversation wasn't strained any longer, and she thanked God for that fact. If Tyler was to be a true father to Sammy, he had to be on cordial terms, at least, with the man who'd been both father and grandfather to Sammy since he was born.

What did Daddy think about all this? He'd maintained a careful silence on the subject, and she thought she knew why. Clayton Caldwell was an honorable man. He would never want to betray that he had a negative thought about the man who was Sammy's father.

If Tyler wanted a model of what a father should be, he obviously couldn't use his own. Her heart hurt when she thought of what Tyler had betrayed about his relationship with his father. Given that model, it was a wonder he was even trying.

He *was* trying, and she had to help him. The better a father Tyler was by the time he left the island, the safer she could feel about sending Sammy to spend time with him.

Tyler was leaning forward, arguing some point with her father in a friendly way. She let her gaze linger on the stubborn line of his jaw, the flash of interest in his eyes, the vigor of his movement when he gestured. The same determination to succeed that had fueled twenty-year-old Tyler's will to take over the company when his father died could make him succeed at fatherhood.

She had to help him, and that meant she had to let him take equal responsibility for both the joys and difficulties of raising Sammy. That meant no more unilateral decisions about her son. She suspected Tyler could never guess just how difficult that was for her.

*Help me with this one, Lord. I'm not good at sharing where Sammy is concerned. Next to You, Daddy will be the best model of a father Tyler is likely to find. Please, open his heart to Daddy and to You.*

The screen door creaked, and Sammy bounded onto the porch. He made a beeline for Tyler, who stopped what he was saying to smile at him.

"What's up?"

Sammy grabbed the arm of the rocker. "Well, I was thinking about when we could go back to Angel Isle to look for the dolphin again. You and Momma said we'd go again, remember?"

"I remember." Tyler tousled Sammy's hair, and their son grinned. "And if I'd forgotten, I'm sure you'd remind me."

"I was thinking we could go this weekend. If we went on Saturday, we'd have lots of time."

She'd half hoped Sammy had forgotten about this. Clearly her son had inherited his father's single-minded determination.

"Sammy, you know that folks have looked for the dolphin for a long time without finding it," her father said. "Seems like maybe we'll have to get used to doing without it."

Sammy shook his head. "I just think maybe I'm going to be the one to find it. And think how happy Great-Gran will be."

Sadness touched her father's eyes. "I guess she would be, at that."

"So could we go on Saturday?" He rocked back and forth on his toes, all energy and stubbornness.

"I suppose—" she began.

"Maybe we can find some day other than this Saturday," Tyler said.

Startled, she met his eyes and realized she'd just done what she'd promised herself she wouldn't do—she'd started to make a decision without consulting him. She'd have to unlearn the habits of the past eight years to make this work.

"Do you have something else planned for Saturday?" She hoped he could see the apology in her eyes.

"Actually, I was hoping you and Sammy would spend Saturday and Sunday in Charleston with me."

"Charleston?" In all the days he'd gone off to the city, it had never occurred to her that he'd want them to go along.

Tyler looked from her to their son. "The manager of our Charleston subsidiary invited us to come and spend the weekend. He has a boy just about your age." He touched Sammy lightly. "Sammy could stay with him and his sitter while we go with Dan and Sheila to a charity concert. It's to raise money for Habitat for Humanity." He waited for Miranda's response.

She sat immobile for a moment. It was a good thing she hadn't blurted her first reaction, because that would have been a resounding no.

Part of the problem was that she knew exactly what benefit concert Tyler was talking about—a huge, expensive, dressy affair for the cream of Charleston society. People with whom Tyler would feel right at home. And she would feel about as welcome as a skunk at a picnic.

She couldn't say any of the things she was thinking in front of her father and Sammy. She summoned a smile. "Let me think about it, okay?"

Eyes questioning, he nodded.

She turned to Sammy, who didn't look thrilled at the idea, either. "Sugar, you have next Monday off from school for a teacher in-service day. Why don't we plan to go then? We can take a picnic lunch, and we'll have all afternoon to do a good search."

The pout that hovered on Sammy's face disappeared. "Can we build a fire and cook hot dogs on it?"

"I don't see why not." The way to a growing boy's heart must be through his stomach.

"Okay. I'm going to tell Theo. I'll bet he'll wish

the high school had a day off, too.'' He darted inside, the screen door slamming.

Before she could muster a reasonable excuse for delaying an answer on the trip to Charleston, her father leaned forward, pressing his palms against the rocker's arms.

''I thought for sure that boy would forget about looking for the dolphin with all the other things that are going on.''

''He's certainly obsessed with it.'' Tyler's gaze met hers, and she knew what he was thinking. He was afraid Sammy had a reason besides pleasing Gran for his search.

''The dolphin's brought us enough sorrow.'' The lines deepened in her father's face. ''I hate to see another generation get caught up in the trouble my brother and I caused.''

''It wasn't your fault,'' she said quickly. ''You didn't take the dolphin, Uncle Jeff did.''

''He took it, but I'm just as much to blame for what followed.''

''But—''

''Hush, Miranda. I mean what I say. I took that grievance against my brother and added it to all the other things I thought he'd done wrong. Told myself I'd bailed him out for the last time.''

''That's understandable.'' She hated that Tyler was hearing this. ''You were the one who was hurt.''

He shook his head. ''I never really gave Jeff a chance after that. I judged him without even realizing I was doing it. And every time he did something I thought was wrong, I just added it to that scale I was making.''

"Daddy, it's not your fault that Uncle Jeff is the way he is." He was expressing feelings she'd never guessed at, and doing it in front of Tyler, of all people. "Anyway, things are better between you now, aren't they?''

"Better." He stood. "Maybe that's what helped me see that I'd done as much wrong in judging him as he'd ever done." He smacked the bad leg he'd had ever since the night the dolphin vanished. "My attitude toward my brother hurt me as much as this leg ever did.''

She could feel the tears sparkle in her eyes, and she blinked them back. "I never knew you felt that way. I just thought—''

"You just thought your uncle Jeff was a man without honor, 'cause that's what you've heard me say. But if Jeff was at fault, I was, too. Maybe if I'd stayed his friend and brother like I should have, I'd have helped him to be a man our momma and daddy would have been proud of.''

Before she could say anything else, he stalked into the house.

She wiped an errant tear away with her fingers. Not speaking, Tyler got up from his chair and came to sit on the swing next to her. It rocked with his movement, then settled.

"All these years, and I never knew he felt that way," she said softly.

Tyler stretched his arm along the swing behind her. It felt strong and secure.

"Your father's an honest man. Not many people would hold themselves to that standard of conduct."

"No, they wouldn't." Did she dare believe he admired her father's character?

"About the dolphin." He hesitated, frowning. "We probably ought to talk about this. About what's behind Sammy's determination to find it."

Was Sammy hoping the dolphin could bring his parents together again? She'd wrestled with it, and she didn't have an answer.

If that was what Sammy wanted, he would think the dolphin was already working if he saw them sitting so close to each other.

She tried to discern Tyler's expression in the dusk. How awkward he must find this situation. It would be even more awkward if he knew what her heart was telling her.

"Maybe we ought to talk to him about the whole thing," she said.

"That's what I thought at first," he said slowly. An expression she couldn't identify crossed his face. "Now I'm thinking that might be a mistake."

"But if he's imagining we're going to get back together if he finds the dolphin—"

"What if he's not thinking anything of the kind? What if this is a complication we've imagined that's never even occurred to him?"

She stared at her hands, twisted together in her lap. "If we bring it up, he'll certainly think about it then."

"Exactly. We might be starting a problem instead of solving it."

"So what do you suggest we do about it?" She looked at him, troubled.

"Let's not say anything for the moment."

His hand rested lightly on her shoulder, and she could feel the weight of his arm across her back. She let herself imagine he was sending out messages of protection and caring.

"If that is what he's thinking, maybe he'll bring it up himself when we go back to the cottage," he went on. "If not, well, we'll have to deal with it once he's convinced the dolphin is gone for good."

She wanted to argue, but she hesitated. She'd promised herself she'd share responsibility for decisions involving Sammy. Now she had a chance to prove she meant it.

"All right," she said reluctantly. "We'll do it your way."

# Chapter Eleven

If someone had told him three weeks ago he'd be driving a rattletrap van down a Georgia back road to buy a bicycle for his son's birthday, he'd have thought that person was hallucinating. Tyler stretched, pressing his hands against the steering wheel.

"This thing isn't exactly built for comfort, is it?"

Miranda smiled, as if at some level she enjoyed his fish-out-of-water discomfort. "We couldn't have fit the bike in your rental car very easily, could we?"

"Guess you have a point there." At least he'd been able to convince her to let him drive. He gave her a sideways glance. Miranda looked less wary today, as if she might almost enjoy this trek with him to buy their son's birthday present.

She hadn't given him an answer yet on going to Charleston on the weekend. He sensed her reluctance without understanding it. With a little luck and tact, on today's expedition he could prove to her that they could be in each other's company for two days without coming to blows, especially since Sammy would be with them.

''The shop is just ahead there.'' Miranda pointed to a bright blue cement-block building.

Tyler pushed aside thoughts of the weekend. He'd better concentrate on getting into the bike shop parking lot without hitting any of the numerous potholes. Each one made the van shiver as if it had a bad case of the flu.

Miranda should have better transportation than this. He took a cautious look at that idea, surprised. It wasn't his business or his responsibility what Miranda drove. So where had that impulse come from to buy her a nice, safe vehicle?

She slipped out of the van without waiting for him to open the door and scurried to the shop. He followed, a little amused. She obviously intended to keep him from paying his share if she could.

That had to be a first in his adult life. Most people were only too ready to let the Winchester bank account foot any bill.

Not Miranda. All those years of raising Sammy without his support—how on earth had she managed? Her family had helped, obviously, but as far as he could tell, Clayton and Sallie were just getting by.

By the time he reached Miranda, the salesman was showing her a bright red bicycle, and she was reaching for her bag.

He caught her hand, stilling the movement. ''Let's have a look first.''

For an instant she pulled against his grip. Then she stopped, maybe realizing how childish that was. She nodded toward the shiny bike. "What do you think of it?"

He surveyed the two-wheeler, wondering how many years it had been since he'd ridden one and what exactly they should look for in a bike for a just-turned-eight-year-old. "Are you sure the wider tires are what he wants?"

"That question proves you haven't ridden a bike on the island lately. You have to have wide tires to make it through the sand." She grinned. "That's why old Mary Lou works so well. You could take back those disparaging remarks about her any time now."

That lighthearted smile reminded him of the younger Miranda. "I'll have to take your word for it. I haven't done much bicycling lately. What about a helmet?"

The salesman jumped in immediately. "We have a nice selection of children's helmets right over here."

Miranda hesitated. "I think there's an old one in the garage he could use."

He saw into her mind so clearly. She was counting up how much money was in her bag, wondering if she had enough to pay for it.

"I'm getting the helmet, and anything else he needs to go with it."

Her mouth was set. "I just agreed to let you go halves on the bike."

"I have a lot of birthdays to make up for, remember?" he said softly. Her betraying flush told him the shot had gone home. He took her arm. "Let's go look at the helmets."

He hadn't intended to remind her of that today, not

when he was trying to persuade her to go to Charleston for the weekend. They followed the clerk past racks of bicycles. But he could be just as stubborn as she could, and he had a right to get his son whatever he wanted for his birthday.

The salesman, apparently sensing a customer who intended to spend money, got into the spirit of the thing. By the time they'd finished, they'd added not just the helmet but also a biking jersey, water bottle and cage and a pack that fit on the handlebars, just in case Sammy wanted to carry anything with him.

"Will that be all?" The salesman sounded hopeful.

Tyler looked at Miranda. "Sure you won't let me get a new bike for you?"

"My old one is fine." Apparently deciding not to take offense, she let an impish twinkle appear in her eyes. It made her look like Sammy. "What about you? We ought to get a bike for you, so you can ride with Sammy."

She was challenging him, he suspected, but if she thought she'd throw him off track, she was going to be disappointed.

"Good idea." He looked at the salesman. "Let's see something for me."

The salesman practically rubbed his hands together.

He had never known buying a bike could be so complicated. After measurements, consultations with another clerk and Miranda's insistence on a bike suitable for beach riding, they finally had him outfitted. He slapped his credit card on the counter before Miranda could reach for her wallet.

"Put it on this one."

Miranda's jaw set, and she pulled a wallet from her overstuffed shoulder bag. "I'm paying my half."

"Let this be on me." He couldn't help trying to persuade her.

She held out the bills to him, arm stiff. "Take it."

He tried to remember the last time a member of his family had repaid him for something. He couldn't, and he knew suddenly that he'd have been disappointed if Miranda had given in.

Besides, if he wanted her cooperation on the weekend trip, he'd better let her have her way.

"I'll take it, but only if you let me get lunch."

"We don't have to stop for lunch."

"Maybe we don't have to, but I'm hungry. Deal?"

She nodded, pushing the bills into his hand. "If that's what you want."

They each wheeled a bike out to the van. He had to admit, as they loaded their purchases, that it was good they'd brought the van, no matter how decrepit it looked.

"Okay." He slammed the door. "Where's a good place for lunch around here?"

"There are some fast-food places along the highway on the way home."

He opened the door for her before she could grab the handle. "I might settle for fast food if Sammy were along, but I'd prefer something up a step or two."

She smiled suddenly, as if deciding that she didn't have a choice so she might as well get into the spirit of it. "A couple of miles down the road there's a good seafood place."

"Done." He held her elbow while she climbed into the van. "I could eat a horse."

A half-hour later, Tyler looked dubiously at the concoction of pink shrimp in creamy sauce atop a roll the waitress had just put down in front of him. "So this is a shrimp roll."

"Hey, you said you didn't want a fast-food burger." Miranda bit into her sandwich with every sign of pleasure. "Shrimp rolls and sweet potato fries aren't on most fast-food menus."

He took a bite, nodded appreciatively and took another. At least Miranda had lost the mulish look she'd worn while insisting he take the money she offered.

He'd like to insist she accept all the support he'd missed out on the past eight years, but he was getting to know this grown-up version of the girl he'd married, and he knew she wouldn't accept. One step at a time, that was the way to get what he wanted.

Now if he could just be sure what that was, he'd be all right.

Miranda set her iced tea glass on the blue-and-white checked tablecloth. Sweet tea, she'd called it. Another low-country thing, like shrimp rolls and sweet potato fries, he assumed.

"Did you manage to get things settled back at the office?" she said.

Are you going away? That was probably what she really wanted to ask him.

"I had a long conversation with Henry. He seems to think Josh is just nervous because he's not used to my being out of the office, especially when a big deal is pending.''

She paused, roll halfway to her mouth. ''Do you trust Henry's opinions?''

That startled him. He wasn't sure Henry, the perfect subordinate, *had* opinions.

''I trust Henry to do what I've instructed him to do. I've gone over every step of the deal with him, and I see no reason anything should go wrong.''

''It's all right, then.''

''Yes.'' He tried to ignore the niggling feeling of doubt. ''I'll talk with both Henry and Josh every day. By next Thursday it'll be settled. The deal we're offering is a good one. The buyers won't get the quality of product we supply at a better price from anyone else.''

He glanced out the window at the marsh grasses bending in the breeze. What was he doing here when he had a deal pending? The Tyler Winchester he'd been a month ago wouldn't have been caught dead anywhere but in the office, personally supervising every step of the deal.

But that Tyler Winchester hadn't known he had a child. Sammy changed things, and Tyler was still trying to understand how.

Which reminded him of the answer he wanted. ''Have you made a decision about going to Charleston with me on Saturday?''

Her lashes swept down, hiding her eyes. ''Why is it so important to you?''

He reached across the table to grasp her hands, making her look at him. ''This is for Sammy. I want him to see that I have another existence besides that of visiting dad. That's a reasonable request, isn't it?''

She looked as if she'd like to say no. ''I suppose so. But we wouldn't have to go to that benefit concert to show Sammy that. All of Charleston society will be there.''

''Is that what's bothering you?'' Why hadn't he realized that? ''You'll do fine. You'll probably be the prettiest woman there.''

''I won't fit in.'' She looked startled that she'd said it to him. ''That sounds silly to you, I guess, but it's true.''

He didn't understand the emotion that lay beneath her words, but it warned him to proceed carefully.

''Not silly,'' he said, clasping her hands. ''But it is surprising. I haven't seen you lacking any confidence in dealing with strangers. That's what you do all the time at the inn, after all.''

''That's different.'' Her hands twisted in his, but she didn't seem aware of the convulsive movement. ''The inn is home. Believe me, I have vivid memories of how I didn't fit in when we were married. It's not an experience I'd care to repeat.''

It was the first time she'd spoken willingly of their marriage. He forced his mind to the couple of months that had changed both of their lives.

''I'm sorry,'' he said slowly. ''Maybe I was oblivious, but I didn't realize the social side of things bothered you that much.''

''I was eighteen.'' She yanked her hands free, anger flaring in her eyes. ''I'd never been farther from home than Savannah. Of course it bothered me. I felt like a failure the whole time I was in Baltimore.''

"Miranda—'' She obviously had painful memories he hadn't even guessed at. "I didn't realize. I'm sorry I was so blind to what you felt.''

Her brief flash of anger went out. "Forget it.''

He didn't want to forget. He wanted to explain it in some way that would get both of them off the hook.

"My father's death pitched both of us into something we weren't ready for.''

She tried an unconvincing smile. "There's no point in going over something that happened a lifetime ago. We were different people then.''

"That's my point. You're not eighteen now. You have enough poise and maturity to run the inn and raise our son. You can take on a few of my business associates, can't you?''

Her smile turned a bit more genuine. "You sound like Gran.''

That seemed highly unlikely. "What did your grandmother say?''

"That I was a Caldwell woman, and they're not afraid of anything. They took on the island and tamed it back when it was the wild frontier.'' She gave a little laugh. "I told her I'd rather tackle an alligator than a society party, and she said that was the point. That the thing I feared was my frontier.''

"Your grandmother's a wise woman.''

"She is.'' Miranda's gaze swept up to touch his face. "I don't want to disappoint her. So I guess I'll be going on Saturday.''

His fingers closed over hers again. "I'm glad.''

He felt unreasonably exhilarated at having gotten his way. But if Miranda was this skittish about a weekend in Charleston, what would she say if he broached the subject that had been hovering in the back of his mind for the past day or two?

What would Miranda say if he told her he thought the best way of taking care of Sammy was for them to get married again?

Tyler should look as out of place as a duck at a wedding, and instead he looked perfectly at ease as he guided her cousin Matt's blindfolded youngest toward the piñata they'd hung from the dining room archway.

Well, she'd wanted him to be comfortable with the whole family here for Sammy's birthday party. She just hadn't expected him to find it that easy.

After their trip the day before to pick up the bicycle, they seemed to have moved to a different level of understanding. She was still trying to figure out what it was.

"You've got to give the man credit." Her sister, Chloe, stopped pouring lemonade long enough to nod toward Tyler. "He's trying."

"Tyler doesn't just try," she said. He was holding the toddler up so she could get in a good swing with the plastic bat. "He stayed off the phone and away from the computer all day, he helped me decorate, he even gave Daddy a hand with the pork barbecue. He's being so perfect it makes me want to scream."

Chloe laughed, her lively face filled with the serenity it had acquired since her marriage to Luke

Hunter. "Honey, perfection is usually considered a good thing in a man."

"I keep trying to remind myself why I'm no longer Mrs. Tyler Winchester," she said with mock severity. "It doesn't help to have everyone singing his praises all of a sudden."

"Singing his praises?" Chloe raised her eyebrows. "Sugar, that doesn't sound like the brothers I know and love."

"Well, maybe not the twins," she admitted. "But even they said he wasn't half bad after he took over hanging the decorations so they didn't have to."

"So what's wrong?" Chloe slipped an arm around Miranda's waist. "Don't you want Sammy's dad to get along with everyone?"

Was she really being that selfish? "I suppose so," she said. "It just makes me wonder what he's up to."

Chloe gave her a squeeze. "Never look a helpful man or a gift horse in the mouth." She picked up the tray of glasses. "I never do."

But Chloe was secure in the love of the man who'd been meant for her. And Miranda was…nervous.

Nervous about this suddenly charming and cooperative Tyler. Nervous about the weekend in Charleston she'd committed herself to. And nervous about what the future held.

*Please.* She snatched a moment for what Gran always called a prayer on the run. *Let this family gathering show Tyler what Sammy has here. Let him understand that he can't make big changes in Sammy's life.*

That sounded like she was telling God what to do

rather than asking for His guidance. Still, she clung to her plea stubbornly. She did know what was best for Sammy, didn't she?

She batted away one of the helium-filled balloons that floated around the room, bumping on the ceiling. A huge balloon bouquet had arrived unexpectedly that morning with a card signed Uncle Josh. Sammy had looked astonished.

"Do I have an uncle Josh?"

"That's my brother," Tyler had explained.

Now that she thought of it, Tyler had looked almost as surprised as Sammy. Apparently he hadn't expected this of his brother.

The piñata split open. Candy and small toys scattered on the floor. Tyler stood back, watching with a smile as the kids rushed to snatch them up.

Then he looked at her, the smile lingering, growing softer, more personal.

It was as if he'd reached across the room and touched her cheek. A wave of warmth swept over Miranda, and her fingers fumbled with the candles she was putting on the cake.

Tyler worked his way through the horde of small children to her side. "Can I help you with that?"

She handed him the candles. "You do it. I seem to be all thumbs."

He arranged candles on the huge sheet cake decorated with dolphins and seashells. "Quite a party. Do you always go all out for birthdays?"

"Well, only the kids get piñatas, but everyone gets a party. It's a good excuse for cake and ice cream."

He frowned, adjusting the position of one candle as if it displeased him. "Another tradition, in fact."

"I guess so. All families have birthday traditions, don't they?"

"I don't know. I was always away at boarding school on my birthday. My mother sent a gift, but that was about all."

At Tyler's mention of boarding school, she felt as if a cold draft had blown through the room, extinguishing the candles.

"You...you're not thinking of boarding school for Sammy, are you?" She could never agree to that.

He straightened, the smile wiped from his face. "I did think that at first. It's what seems natural to me. My brother and I never questioned that we'd go off to boarding school when we were eight."

Her heart cramped at the thought of the boy he'd been. "I couldn't let you do that to Sammy."

"Relax. I've given up that idea." He glanced around the room. "Sammy shouldn't be away from family."

She could breathe again. "I'm glad you see that."

He frowned, his dark eyes serious. "That doesn't mean I'll let you have everything your way. Sammy has to learn to be a part of the outside world, too."

"Is that what this trip to Charleston is?" Fear made her voice sharp. "Some kind of test to see how Sammy does there?"

"Of course not." His voice was even sharper than hers, and the cooperative Tyler who'd been around all day seemed to vanish. "Don't put words in my mouth, Miranda. I've already told you—I just want

Sammy to see the world I function in, because someday he'll have to function there, too.''

''It didn't work very well when I tried it.'' Apprehension about the weekend forced the words out.

That reminder seemed to rattle him. For a moment
she didn't think he'd reply, but then he shook his
head, face somber.

''I admit I didn't do a good job of introducing you
to my world, Miranda. But then, you never really tried
to fit in, did you?''

''That's not fair.'' She lowered her voice to a furious whisper. ''I didn't have the least idea what I
was getting into, and you didn't help.''

''We both made mistakes.'' He spoke quietly, although no one in the chattering crowd could possibly
hear them. ''We were both too young to do it right.''
His hand closed around her wrist, and her pulse thundered against his palm. ''I won't make the same mistake with our son. I promise you that.''

She wasn't sure whether to consider that a promise
or a threat.

# Chapter Twelve

"**M**iranda looks upset." Gran Caldwell planted herself in front of Tyler, letting the party swirl around them. Her voice was tart, and her eyes snapped at Tyler.

He glanced toward the table where Miranda and her sister were rapidly cutting cake and passing pieces out. He could protest that she was busy with the birthday party, but he suspected a half-truth wouldn't sit well with Miranda's grandmother.

"We had a misunderstanding." He tried not to let exasperation show in his voice. Didn't Miranda see that he had a right to expose their son to the wider world?

"Be better for Sammy if his parents understood each other."

Miranda's grandmother certainly had a point there. It was what he believed, too. Unfortunately, every time he thought he and Miranda were reaching that point, some unwary remark opened a chasm between them.

The buzz of conversation and the high voices of the children effectively masked anything he and Mrs. Caldwell might say to each other. Still, he wasn't sure he wanted to be having this talk with her.

"We're still trying to figure out how to deal with this situation," he said. How impolite would it be to slip away from the lecture Miranda's grandmother undoubtedly had in mind?

The frilly pink party hat that sat atop Gran's coronet of gray hair bobbed. "I reckon it's not easy. But then, change never is."

He glanced at her, a little surprised by the comment. "I wouldn't have thought change was something that came very often to Caldwell Island. Everywhere I turn, I trip over one tradition or another."

"Change comes to everybody, no matter where they live." She patted a child who ran by, but her gaze was still focused on him. "Caldwell Island might look the same to you as it did eight years ago, but it's changed beyond all recognition since I was a girl."

"I suppose it has." This elderly woman couldn't imagine the changes that took place daily in the world he lived in.

"You're thinking I don't know a thing about how you live."

Her perception startled him again, and he could see she knew that and enjoyed it.

"I didn't mean to offend you."

She patted his arm, her heavily veined hand surprisingly strong. "You don't have to worry about being polite to me, son. You just have to worry about doing your best for Sammy and Miranda."

"The tricky part is deciding just what the best is." That was the thought that haunted him, but he surprised himself by saying it to her.

"Our Miranda has strong feelings about raising her son."

Gran Caldwell looked across the room, and he followed her gaze to where Miranda was seating children around the oval wooden table they'd covered with a bright red birthday cloth. She was passing out plates of cake and simultaneously refereeing some dispute.

The denim skirt and aqua shirt Miranda wore outlined her slender figure. Come to think of it, he hadn't seen her wear anything that didn't look good on her. Not stylish, maybe, and certainly not expensive, but that didn't seem to matter.

"She comes from a long line of strong women." Gran's eyes twinkled. "Opinionated, too."

"I've noticed that." His lips creased in an unwilling smile. The woman had him, and she knew it.

She patted his arm again with what he might imagine was affection. "Talk to her. She'll listen if she knows you respect her opinion. You can't understand each other if you're not willing to do that."

Apparently having said what she intended to, Miranda's grandmother moved off. He let his gaze drift to Miranda again.

She had stepped back a little from the table, letting her father snap a photo of Sammy with his cake. Her gaze rested on their son, and he saw a vulnerability in her expression that he hadn't recognized before.

Strong, yes. Her grandmother was right about that. But Miranda was vulnerable, too, in spite of being surrounded by people who loved her. Whether she knew it or not, she needed a man to share things with, a man she could depend on.

And how exactly did that fit into the idea he had been struggling with for the last few days—the thought that he and Miranda should marry again?

That would be best for Sammy, wouldn't it? He'd have both his parents, and he wouldn't have to feel split between them.

They'd need to work something out so that Sammy and Miranda still spent plenty of time on the island. He knew Miranda would never agree to anything else. Besides, he'd grown to respect the heritage his son had here.

Marriage would affect him and Miranda, too, obviously, as well as Sammy. As for himself, he'd decided a long time ago that marriage wasn't for him. He'd never settle for the kind of relationship his parents had had, and his attempt to create something different with Miranda had ended in a dismal failure.

He couldn't offer Miranda that fairy-tale romance they'd once thought they could have. He wasn't even sure such a thing existed.

Probably even happily married people like Miranda's parents eventually settled for mutual respect and friendship. Wasn't it reasonable for him and Miranda to start out that way the second time around?

This could be right for all three of them, but he

had to move cautiously. Miranda's grandmother had it right—he and Miranda had to understand each other before they could forge a new relationship. He had to be patient.

Unfortunately, patience wasn't one of his better qualities. He was used to choosing a goal and charging toward it, pushing aside anything that stood in his way.

He imagined the weekend trip to Charleston as a positive step toward making Miranda see that they should be together as a family. If that were going to happen, he had to make peace with her right now.

He worked his way across the room, dodging the sticky hands of several small Caldwell cousins who'd escaped from the cake table. Miranda was trying to make room for a tray of glasses.

"Let me take that." He grasped the metal tray and put it down on the space she cleared. She shot him a glance of thanks, followed by instant wariness.

She was still thinking about their last conversation, obviously. If he wanted this to work, he had to clear that up.

"Can we talk?"

Her steady gaze assessed him, then she nodded. "Yes, if you can talk while carrying the coffee in."

"I can do that."

He followed her through the door to the kitchen. It swung shut, cutting off the party clamor. The ensuing quiet was so startling his ears rang.

Miranda picked up another tray, this one filled with cups. "I'll take this in, if you can bring the coffee urn."

Indian River Area Library
3546 S. Straits Hwy.
P.O. Box 160

He put his hands over hers, setting the tray on the scrubbed pine table. "Wait just a second. Please," he added.

"Whatever it is, can't it wait?" She tried to pull away, but he held her hands fast.

"Nobody's in that much of a hurry for coffee. You can give me a minute."

Her green eyes turned stormy, but she nodded. "All right. A minute."

"I'm sorry."

Her hands stilled in his. "For what?"

"That conversation we had about going to Charleston—I said it all wrong."

She was listening to him. He could let go of her hands. He didn't want to.

"I understand. You want Sammy to go so he can see what kind of circles you move in." Again that hint of vulnerability showed.

"I want the two of you to come so we can have a good time together," he said firmly. "And I suppose I do want Sammy to see me on my own turf. That's not such a bad thing, is it?"

"Are you saying I overreacted?" Her lips curved in the beginning of a reluctant smile.

The tension inside him eased. She was going to listen. "Maybe just a little."

"Okay." She let out a breath that was almost a sigh. "You're right. Sammy should see you in a situation where you feel comfortable."

Her comment startled him. Had he been acting uncomfortable?

"I like it here, Miranda. But we are kind of surrounded by family."

"Especially today." The corners of her eyes crinkled. "I know. You deserve some alone time with Sammy off the island and away from hordes of Caldwells."

He smoothed his thumb over her knuckles. "So we'll go?"

Her lashes swept down to hide her eyes, but she nodded.

"We'll have a good time, I promise." They would. He'd make sure of that.

Miranda would begin to see that they belonged together as a family. Maybe what he had to offer wasn't a fairy-tale romance, but it would be good enough.

She had to learn to cope with Tyler's world, or Sammy wouldn't feel comfortable there. So this weekend was the challenge she had to face, no matter how she dreaded it. Miranda looked out the car window, watching signs and consulting the map as Tyler negotiated the narrow streets of downtown Charleston.

"Turning left at the next corner will take us toward the Battery."

Tyler nodded, his face, in profile, relaxed. City traffic clearly wasn't the monster to him that it had always been to her.

"I want to take a picture of the cannons." Sammy leaned as far forward in the back seat as his seat belt would permit, brandishing the disposable camera his father had bought him for the trip. "I can take my pictures to school, can't I?"

"Sure you can," Tyler said. "We'll make sure we get lots of them."

Everything about him seemed at ease. As he'd said, he was on his own turf here. Charleston might not be that familiar to him, but it was a city, and the people they'd encounter were his colleagues.

They'd arranged to sightsee during the day, then go to Dan and Sheila Carpenter's house in time to dress for dinner and the charity concert. Her stomach clenched at the thought, and she chastised herself for being such a wimp. The Carpenters were just people, after all.

The truth was, she was still a daughter in her father's house, still living the simple life she'd always known. Gran had been right about that—Caldwell Island wasn't a frontier for her.

She would find a way to adapt to this situation. She had to, for Sammy's sake. It didn't have anything to do with her relationship with Tyler, just Sammy. She sat up a little straighter. She could do anything for her son.

"There's a parking lot." She pointed. "I'm sure we can walk down to the Battery from here."

Tyler pulled into the gravel lot, taking a ticket from the automatic dispenser. He gave her a quick smile. "Good navigating, Miranda."

She folded the city map and slipped it into her bag. "I don't mind reading the map, but I surely don't like driving in the city."

"Charleston is a challenge. These streets must not have been widened since horse-and-carriage days."

"No, I suppose they haven't." The narrow streets, lined with elegant antebellum houses and pocket gardens tucked behind wrought-iron fences, seemed to take them a step back in time.

They got out, Sammy checking to be sure he had his camera and baseball cap.

"Did you know the War Between the States started at Fort Sumter?" Sammy fell in step with his father.

Tyler smiled at him. "I assume you mean the Civil War?"

Sammy grinned. "Don't let Gran hear you call it that."

The ease of their exchange warmed Miranda's heart. Whatever the future held, this was how the relationship should be between Sammy and his daddy. Her son deserved what she had with her father. It had never been right to try to keep Sammy and Tyler apart.

*I thought I was doing the right thing, Lord. Teach me how to look at myself more clearly. Show me how to make up for my mistakes.*

She caught a glimpse of water ahead, and in a few minutes they'd emerged onto the wide walk and wall of the Battery. Out in the harbor, the twin forts that once protected the city had, no doubt, been invaded by tourists. The breeze from the water lifted her hair.

"Cannons," Sammy said with satisfaction, pointing to the black cannons that lined the Battery. "I knew there'd be cannons."

"Looks like there are some soldiers, too." Tyler

nodded to two young men in gray uniforms who leaned against the wall.

"They're Citadel cadets," Sammy said knowledgeably. "I thought I'd like to go to the Citadel when I get big enough, but Uncle David says if I want to study dolphins, like he does, I should go where he went to school in Florida. Then I can be an…an oceanographer." He said the long word carefully.

They reached the wall, and Tyler leaned against it, looking at their son. "Is that what you want to be, an oceanographer?"

Was that disapproval in his voice? She couldn't be sure. It might be, if Tyler envisioned Sammy taking over the company for him one day.

Sammy shrugged. "I dunno. Maybe." He swung the camera up. "I'm going to take a picture of the cannon." He darted off.

Tyler watched him run along the walkway. "That is one smart kid we have."

"Of course he is." She leaned against the wall next to him. She didn't know whether or not to be offended that Tyler would even think he had to say it.

He focused on her, smiling. "Don't get huffy. I just meant I'd probably never heard the word oceanographer when I was his age."

"Well, Sammy's grown up with the sea. You had other interests."

Tyler shook his head, the smile fading a little as he stared at the water. He'd rolled back his sleeves, and his forearms were tanned against the cream-colored shirt. Seagulls swooped, wings sparkling in the sunlight.

"You mean my father had other interests. My future was predetermined. I had to take over the company. He just never thought it would happen as soon as it did."

"Is that what you hope for Sammy?" She forced her voice to be steady. "That he'll take over the company one day?"

"I confess the thought crossed my mind when I met him. Why wouldn't it?"

Before she could protest, he touched her hand where it rested on the wall.

"I know what you're going to say, and you needn't bother. Sammy gets to determine his own future. Whatever he wants to be is all right with me."

"I'm glad you feel that way." *Thank you, Lord. That was one battle I didn't want to fight.*

"I don't want to be the kind of father mine was." His fingers closed over hers, and she felt the warmth all the way up her arm. "Unfortunately I don't have any other models."

"You'll learn by doing," she said, knowing it was true. "That's all any of us can do."

Just as she would learn to cope with his world by doing—beginning by staying with his friends and attending a social event. That was the only way she could help Sammy in the difficult adjustments he'd have to make when he started living with Tyler part of the time.

"Daddy, come see the cannon," Sammy called. "I want to take your picture."

"You've got it." Tyler pushed away from the wall. He caught her hand as they walked toward their son, and she steeled herself for the inevitable tingle as their hands swung, palm to palm.

It doesn't mean anything, she told herself desperately. Tyler has made that clear.

"You stand there with Momma." Sammy pushed them into place next to the cannon. "I'll take a picture."

The cadets strolled by, and one of them stopped, smiling at Sammy. "Would you like me to take it so you can be in it, too?"

Sammy gave him an awestruck look, then nodded. "Thank you, sir. That would be very nice."

He handed over the camera and scurried to pose next to his father. Tyler put his hand on their son's shoulder, linking them.

A family portrait, she thought as the cadet snapped one picture, then another. We might be any happy family out for the day.

Her smile faltered at the pain in her heart. Her goal—learning to function in Tyler's world to help Sammy—suddenly seemed a poor substitute for what she really wanted. For what she knew she'd never have.

They'd never be the happy family of the photo, because that wasn't what Tyler wanted any longer.

"This is the house." Tyler parked at the curb on the cobblestone street. "You'll like the Carpenters." At least, he hoped she would. He could feel Miranda's nervousness from across the front seat.

He clasped her hand for an instant, telling himself he was only trying to convey assurance that this visit would be all right. He seemed to be doing that often lately—making an excuse to himself to touch her.

He got out, and Sammy came quickly to help him as he unloaded the bags.

"Look, Sammy. It's a genuine Charleston historic home." Miranda nodded at the bronze plaque set into the faded brick wall.

Tyler pushed open the filigree wrought-iron gate in the brick wall, and they stepped into a lush green garden with azaleas in full bloom. The house ran along the left side of the garden, and the brick walls lined the other sides, creating an oasis in the midst of the city.

A fountain with a graceful seahorse spout sprayed water in an arc, catching and reflecting a ray of sunshine that filtered through the sheltering live oaks.

"I've never seen anything quite like this." Tyler set down the bags on the brick walk to close the gate. "It's beautiful."

Miranda's face had tightened. "Yes. Your friends have a lovely home."

Sammy had run ahead to peer into the fountain, but Tyler lowered his voice anyway. "Why does it bother you? Your uncle's house is probably just as big."

"It's not the same. People don't live in a house like this unless they're part of Charleston society."

"Maybe Dan is from an old Charleston family. It doesn't matter. This is just business."

What was she thinking? That this would be as difficult as those weeks in Baltimore had been?

She nodded, but the tense line of her jaw told him that his rationalization didn't really help.

He clasped her elbow as they moved up the walk, hoping she knew he was on her side. But then, why would she feel any assurance of that? He should have been on her side when he'd taken her to Baltimore as his bride, and he hadn't been able to help her then.

No, that was letting himself off too easy. He looked back with disgust at the callow boy he'd been then. He'd been so obsessed with filling his father's shoes that he hadn't given a thought to how his decisions affected Miranda. He should have known, he should have done better, he should have been smarter.

They'd both been too young when they fell in love, and they hadn't known how to make it work. Now it was too late. He couldn't offer her what he should have then, but he certainly could make an effort to see that she felt comfortable here.

"It's business," he said again as they stepped onto the piazza. "You'll find both Dan and Sheila eager to make us welcome."

She glanced up with a flicker of a smile. "Because you're the big boss, you mean."

The smile encouraged him. "Oh, I'm an important person, all right." He lifted an eyebrow, holding her arm in a firm clasp. "Ready?"

She nodded, and he reached out to let the brass knocker fall.

Sheila Carpenter opened the door at once. "Come in, come in." Her wide smile swept them into a cool, elegant hallway. "We've been waiting for you."

"It's good to see you again, Sheila."

He glanced around, trying to see what Miranda might find intimidating about the place. The spiral staircase that swirled upward without apparent support might take his breath away, and the portraits on the walls might be antebellum ancestors, but otherwise it was just a house.

"We're just so happy to have y'all here." Sheila clasped Miranda's hand. Tall and blond, she was as elegant as her home, but genuine welcome shone in her wide blue eyes.

"It's very kind of you to invite us." There was no trace of nervousness showing in the warmth of her response.

"Our boy, Todd, is looking forward to having a guest." Sheila smiled at Sammy. "This must be Sammy."

Sammy shook hands with a grave courtesy that seemed inborn.

Tyler glanced from his son to Miranda. They both had that innate courtesy and dignity. With that and her native intelligence, Miranda could fit in anywhere. She just didn't seem to have confidence in that fact.

She'd had it, once upon a time. His memory flashed him an image of the girl Miranda had been when he'd met her. She'd had such natural grace and such bright confidence. She'd been willing to take on anything. She'd lost that somewhere along the way.

No, not somewhere. She'd lost it when he'd swept her into a marriage neither of them had been ready for.

The guilt he'd denied for years burst out of hiding. Their marriage and what had happened to her as a result had robbed Miranda of her girlhood, her college education, her chance at the happy family she deserved.

What could he offer her that would make up for that?

# *Chapter Thirteen*

Miranda took a deep breath, opened the bedroom door and stepped into the upstairs hall of the Carpenters' house. She sank almost to her ankles, it seemed, in plush carpet.

Tyler waited under the amber glow of the wall sconces. He looked at her, not speaking, a portrait in black and white with his dark hair and dark eyes, his white shirtfront and black tuxedo.

She smoothed her hands nervously down the black silk of the evening pantsuit her sister had insisted she borrow.

"Well? Is this outfit all right?" Pitiful, a tiny voice in her mind taunted. You're begging for a compliment from him.

"Very all right." Tyler reached out to touch the curl she'd let fall to her shoulder from her swept-back hair. "You look beautiful."

Begged for or not, his words were good to hear. "It's not me—it's the clothes. Chloe got this outfit for the kickoff party when Dalton Resorts broke ground for the new hotel. She said it would be just right for tonight's concert, but I wasn't sure.''

"Chloe has good taste, but you're wrong." His fingertips trailed from her hair to her cheek, and she had to fight the longing to lean against him.

"I'm wrong about what?" How had her voice gotten so breathless?

"You are beautiful no matter what you wear." He pressed his palm against her cheek, and heat rose to her skin where he touched. "Now just say thank-you instead of arguing."

"Thank you," she whispered, her senses swimming.

This was what she wanted—this kind of relationship with Tyler. She'd been kidding herself to think she could be happy with any less.

"What do you think? Are we all ready to go?" Dan asked the question as he and Sheila came out of a door farther along the hallway.

Sheila looked elegant in cream lace shot through with gold thread. Dan, like Tyler, wore a tuxedo, but to Miranda's eyes he couldn't hold a candle to Tyler's dark good looks.

Tyler nodded. "We're ready, and you and I are lucky. We'll be the envy of every man there."

Sheila laughed as she started down the open spiral staircase. "That's what I like—a man who knows how to turn a compliment."

Tyler took Miranda's hand, slipping it into the crook of his arm. Her fingers closed on hard muscle.

"Smile," he whispered as they reached the top of the staircase. "This evening will be fun."

Fun, she thought, trailing her hand along the polished mahogany railing. This evening with Tyler wasn't fun. It was magical.

She had seen no reason to change her mind by the time they arrived at the restaurant Dan had chosen on Bay Street. Tyler helped her from the car, and she felt like Cinderella alighting from her coach.

He clasped her hand in his, waiting while Dan gave his keys to the valet. "Relax," he murmured softly, his breath brushing her ear as he bent close to her.

Was it conceivable that he thought she could relax when every nerve in her body was on edge at his nearness?

Dan and Sheila led the way through a wrought-iron archway, and they followed the hostess across a cobblestone patio surrounded by gaslights on black iron posts. The lights flickered on boxwood hedges and white tablecloths. String music from some hidden source muted the echo of conversation.

Magical, she thought as they reached a table set for four.

Tyler pulled out her chair. When she sat down, his fingers caressed her shoulders as lightly as the aroma of the flowers caressed her senses. The bowl of camellias in the center of the table seemed to waver for a moment.

"Good choice." Tyler sat next to her, glancing across the linen-covered table at Dan. "You know how to pick a restaurant."

Sheila looked around with satisfaction. "We

thought you'd like it. They're known for doing great things with local fare like shrimp and black-eyed peas, so be sure you try something unique to Charleston.''

The conversation moved to food, giving Miranda a respite to catch her breath and try to slow her tumultuous pulse. What was Tyler up to?

The touches, the sultry glances—they weren't accidental. It was as if he'd set out tonight to remind her of what they'd once had.

She slanted a look at him from behind the protective cover of the menu, and her heart trembled. She didn't need reminders. All she had to do was look at him, and she saw again the husband she'd never stopped loving.

The strong bones of his face were more pronounced, and there were fine lines around his eyes that spoke of the stress of the past years. But one thing hadn't changed—the way her heart stopped when he smiled at her.

"What do you think?" Tyler lowered his menu. "Sullivan Island crab cakes for a starter, followed by pecan-crusted fried shrimp with apricot chutney?"

"Sounds wonderful," she said, trying for normalcy. "I've never met a fried shrimp I didn't like."

"That's it, then." Tyler closed the menu. "We think alike tonight."

He gave her a small, private smile, as if the two of them shared a secret.

Her heart swelled with love. Hopeless, to try to keep her feelings a secret. Her love for Tyler must be shining in her eyes for everyone to see.

\* \* \*

This was the way he'd once imagined their lives would be, Tyler realized as they drove to the house after the concert.

He glanced at Miranda, seated next to him in the back seat of Dan's car. He'd pictured them doing this sort of thing, had envisioned Miranda looking elegant, beautiful and perfectly at ease. Pictured them coming home to their own house with their children asleep in their beds.

It was too late now to think about what might have been once upon a time. He had to concentrate on the present, and the present included a Miranda who'd fit in perfectly and had seemed to enjoy the evening.

At the moment she continued a lively conversation with Sheila about the community's youth center. Apparently the volunteer work she did at the center in Beaufort was similar to what Sheila did in Charleston, and the two of them had been exchanging war stories.

He captured her hand where it lay between them on the leather seat. Her fingers curled around his, and he thought she nearly tripped over a word.

This was working—he was sure of it. Miranda had begun to see that she could function perfectly well in the world he moved in. It would be a small step from that to convincing her that a marital partnership was best for all of them.

"Here we are." Dan pulled into the converted carriage house that served as his garage. "We'll walk in through the garden. Sheila's done a wonderful job with it."

"You're only saying that because you know it's true," Sheila teased.

Tyler kept Miranda's hand securely enclosed in his as they went through a gate in the brick wall that rimmed the back and side of the enclosed garden. He heard her breath catch as they stepped into the garden.

He could understand her response. Tiny white lights, hidden in the shrubbery, picked out the gleam of a camellia here, the blush of an azalea blossom there. Lights illuminated the fountain, making the water glitter like crystal.

"It is perfectly lovely, Sheila." Miranda's voice was soft, as if she didn't want to disturb the night. "I can't imagine anything more charming."

"Well, now, y'all just stay out here and enjoy it for a bit." She grasped Dan's arm and whisked him toward the door. "We'll go up and make sure those boys are asleep, and we'll leave the door unlatched for you. Stay as long as you want."

The door closed behind them, cutting off Dan's surprised comment.

"Sheila's being tactful." He guided Miranda toward a wrought-iron bench that faced the fountain. "She's giving us a chance to be alone."

"I don't think...that is, we've been alone plenty of times." She rushed the words, as if tension danced along her nerves, and sat down abruptly.

"Not in such a romantic setting." He sat next to her, stretching his arm along the seat behind her and letting his hand cup her shoulder.

She sat very straight. "It sounded as if you and Dan were talking business at the intermission."

Obviously Miranda didn't want to discuss how romantic the setting was, though he suspected she couldn't ignore the heavy scent of flowers that perfumed the air. But if it made her feel more comfortable, they'd talk business.

"Dan has ideas about our acquiring some other companies in the southeast. I guess he thought this evening was his best chance to air them."

"Are they good ideas?" She sounded relieved that she'd successfully turned the conversation.

"Fairly good." He tilted his head, staring absently at the spray of water glistening in the light as he considered. "Maybe a little too ambitious for us right now. We have the other deal I told you about pending."

"So you don't intend to go along with his suggestions?" She made it a question.

"He's a good man with a lot of talent," he said slowly.

Funny. He wasn't used to discussing the decisions he made with anyone. That wasn't his style.

But Miranda had her gaze fixed on his face as if this was the most natural thing in the world, and at the moment, it seemed so.

"You don't want to discourage him," she said.

"That's exactly right. Maybe his idea isn't best for us at the moment, but I'd never want to dampen his ingenuity." He drew her a little closer. "You'd make a good manager."

"That comes of being a middle child in a big family," she said lightly. "You learn to manage people or you fight all the time."

"And you don't like to fight."

"I'm not good at it." She sobered suddenly. "Maybe if—"

"Maybe if what?" He wanted to know what had set that frown between her brows.

She gave him a solemn look that was very like Sammy's. "Maybe if I'd been better at fighting, things would have worked out better between us."

He was startled, not so much at the truth of the statement but that she knew both of them well enough to say it to him. "You ran away instead."

"And you didn't chase me."

He caressed the smooth skin of her shoulder. "I should have. I wasn't smart enough to understand what was happening."

Did he understand what was happening now?

The question annoyed him. Of course he did. He was showing Miranda that they had a chance to put their lives together again, the way they should be. They could have a marriage based on common interests and mutual respect.

Somehow the moonlit garden didn't seem the right place to be thinking about common interests. And the sensations he felt at having Miranda in the circle of his arm didn't have anything to do with mutual respect.

"We were too young." She said the words softly, mournfully, as if grieving for someone who'd died.

We're not too young now.

The words hovered on his lips, ready to be spoken, but something held him back. He didn't want to embark on a discussion of the businesslike marriage he envisioned, not here in the moonlight, not in someone else's garden with Dan and Sheila inside wondering what they were doing.

"It doesn't matter now." He turned her face toward him, hand cradling her cheek. "There's no point in dwelling on the past."

His thumb brushed her lips, and he felt them tremble.

"There is a point." Her lashes swept down, then up, unveiling the troubled expression in her eyes. "If you can't forgive me for not telling you about our son, it matters quite a lot."

Her words arrowed straight into his heart and lodged there. "Is that what you think? That I'm still angry with you?"

"Aren't you?"

"No!" Suddenly it seemed the most important thing in the world that she believe him. "I *was* angry at first, but I understand now. Even if I didn't understand, I couldn't have gone on being angry when I saw how much you love our son."

A tear spilled over, glistening on her cheek until he wiped it away with his fingertip.

"Thank you, Tyler. I'm glad."

The soft words, the perfumed air, the warm familiar body next to him wiped away whatever armor he had left against her. He ought to tell her, ought to explain his plans for their future, but all of that was swamped in the need to have her in his arms.

He lowered his head, and his lips found hers. He pulled her close against him.

Miranda settled into his arms as if she'd never left

them. Her mouth was warm and sweet and alive against his, and he never intended to let her get away from him again.

This is going to work. He buried his face in the curve of her neck and felt her arms clasp him tightly. He'd find the right time, he'd explain it all to her, and Miranda would understand.

The fact that they still had such a powerful attraction to each other—well, that made it all the better, didn't it?

Miranda could only wish she knew where they were going. She looked out the car window the next afternoon, watching the thick pine forest slide past. Geographically they were on their way to Caldwell Island. But emotionally where were they headed?

She slid a sideways glance at Tyler. He looked simultaneously relaxed and in control when he drove, as if the mechanical actions freed him from some internal tension that was otherwise present.

He caught her glance and smiled, and her heart turned over in her chest. Well, her emotions certainly weren't in question.

But Tyler's remained a mystery. Even in the turbulent wake of last night's kisses, she wasn't sure of him. The only thing she was sure of, as a result of this weekend, was that she'd faced something she feared and come out okay. Gran had been right, it seemed. She'd grown up.

"Is Sammy still sleeping?" he murmured.

She glanced to the back seat, where Sammy leaned against his seat belt, eyes closed. She nodded. "Those two boys must have stayed up late last night playing.''

''Guess so. They both looked as if they had a hard time staying awake in church this morning.''

She'd been a little surprised when Dan and Sheila had taken it for granted that they'd attend church together. She'd been more surprised when Tyler had agreed without a murmur.

The huge antebellum brick church with its magnificent pulpit and professional choir had been quite a contrast to St. Andrew's, but she'd felt at home there. The message had been just as clear, just as loving as any she'd ever heard.

''I liked the service,'' she ventured, wondering what he was thinking. ''It was nice of Dan and Sheila to invite us to go with them.''

He nodded, frowning. ''I don't think I've ever heard a sermon before on Joseph and his brothers. Or on brothers at all, for that matter.''

Was he thinking about his relationship with his brother? She couldn't be sure, but she felt compelled to keep him talking.

''The pastor did have a good point. The deepest hurt as well as the deepest love happens in families.''

''Maybe so.''

Tyler sounded noncommittal, and it pained her. Could anything ever repair the damage his family had done to him?

She'd be kidding herself if she imagined she might be able to do that. Perhaps his love for Sammy would be enough to heal his pain, as it had once healed hers.

''I've always liked the story of Joseph.'' She didn't

want to let him lapse into silence. "The verse about the brothers intending what happened for evil but God intending it for good—that speaks to me. I guess I need to know that God can bring good out of even the worst of circumstances."

For a moment she thought he wouldn't respond. Then he glanced across at her with a slight smile.

"Your faith must be contagious, you know that? I've thought more about what I believe in the last couple of weeks than I have in a lot of years."

"Coming to any conclusions?" She held her breath, wanting to encourage, not wanting to push.

"Only that I need to do some more thinking."

She smiled, glancing at Sammy as he stirred and pushed himself upright. "That's a good start, don't you think?"

"Maybe so." He looked at Sammy in the rearview mirror. "Hey, sleepyhead. We're almost home."

Sammy blinked and stretched. "I'm glad we went to Charleston. I had a good time, didn't you, Momma?"

"I sure did." Possibly the best part had been the past few minutes. They swept onto the bridge, and as the island came into view, a prayer formed in her heart.

*He's questioning, Lord. Please, draw him back to You for his answers. He'll be a better man and a better father when he grows to know You.*

Whether anything could restore the love Tyler had once felt for her, she didn't know. She did know that restoring his relationship with God was the best thing that could happen to him.

They pulled into the driveway at the inn, and Tyler's cell phone began to ring. Well, they'd had a little time without business. He couldn't seem to get away from it entirely, even on a Sunday.

He put the phone to his ear, taking on what she always thought of as his business expression—absorbed, grave, intent.

She glanced at Sammy. "Grab your bag before you run inside, okay?"

He nodded, then slid quickly out, duffel bag in hand. He looked eager to tell the whole family about his big weekend. She started to follow him, intending to let Tyler take his call in peace.

Tyler caught her arm to stop her, tension communicated through the pressure of his fingers. The monosyllables of his conversation didn't tell her anything, but apprehension slid through her.

Finally he disconnected the call, still frowning.

"What is it? What's wrong?" Unpleasant possibilities chased each other through her mind like black clouds before a storm.

Tyler focused on her, his eyes very dark. "That was the private investigator I hired to find the man who took the picture of Sammy."

Her heart thudded uncomfortably. Whatever the answer was to that mystery, it was bound to create still more questions, maybe more problems. But they couldn't hide from it.

"Did he learn anything?"

"It turns out your mysterious bird-watcher was a bit more than that." Tyler looked angry and perplexed. "He was a private investigator himself."

She stared at him blankly. "A private investigator?" She could only echo his words, trying to get her mind around the concept. "But what— I don't understand. Does that mean someone actually hired him to come here and spy on us? On Sammy?"

"Unless you believe in a huge string of coincidences, that's the most likely thing." Tyler slammed the palm of his hand on the steering wheel. "If I could get my hands on him—"

"Don't, Tyler, don't." Some corner of her heart mourned the disappearance of the peace and hope she'd been feeling since those moments in the moonlit garden the night before.

"Don't what?" He bit off the words.

"I know it's upsetting, but you've got to let the professionals handle it."

He glared for a moment, then gave her a wry smile. "I've always said you should hire the best person for a job and then stay out of the way and let them do it. But in this case—"

"In this case it's too personal," she finished for him. "But we don't really have a choice, do we?"

"No. No matter how much I might want to rampage around Charleston looking for answers, you're right." He clenched his jaw. "He says he should know the rest of it in a day or two."

Apprehension seemed to dig a hole in her heart. "What do you plan to do then?"

"Once I know who's been interfering in our lives, I'll know what to do." His knuckles whitened on the steering wheel. "Whoever he is, he'll be called to account. He's going to regret doing anything to my son.''

Tyler seemed to turn inward, his expression bleak. It was almost as if he'd forgotten she was there.

She ought to be glad one piece of the mystery that surrounded the photograph would be unraveled soon. She shouldn't be thinking about how it was going to affect her relationship with Tyler. But she couldn't seem to help it.

# *Chapter Fourteen*

Tyler frowned at himself in the bedroom mirror the next morning, then transferred the frown to his cell phone, lying atop the dresser. It was probably irrational, but he'd somehow expected to hear from the private investigator this morning. For the amount of money he was paying the firm, he should see faster results than this.

Miranda's face, her eyes troubled, rose in his mind. She'd been as upset as he at learning that someone had apparently hired a private investigator to look into Sammy's parentage. Probably it had hit her harder because in her safe, peaceful little world things like that didn't happen.

If he persuaded her to marry him again, she'd have to learn to expect the unexpected. He knew as well as anyone that the prospect of large amounts of money brought out the worst in most people. There would be money at the bottom of this business with the photograph. He was sure of it.

Miranda didn't think that way, of course. Still, even her bright innocence had been damaged by their brief marriage. How much would she have to change to fit into his world? Would she consider marriage worth what she'd have to sacrifice?

He clutched the cell phone and slid it into his pocket. He wasn't used to doubting himself or his decisions. He most definitely wasn't used to letting someone else take care of something as crucial as finding out the motive behind sending him that photograph.

His edginess could be attributed to that fact, he realized. He hated waiting for someone to call and tell him. He wanted to be involved.

Well, why not? He could go to Charleston, get on the private investigator's back, keep after him until they found out the truth.

Just the idea of doing something positive in this situation energized him. He grabbed a tie and knotted it automatically as he headed out the door. He'd have to let Miranda know what he intended, and then he could be on his way.

His mind raced ahead to the road to Charleston as he trotted down the stairs. He glanced into the dining room. Sallie Caldwell was clearing tables, but Miranda was nowhere in sight.

She was probably in the office. She often used these morning hours to catch up on her book work after the flurry of getting breakfast.

He pushed open the office door. Miranda looked up from a stack of envelopes on the desk, her mouth softening in a smile at the sight of him. The green shirt she wore accentuated the sparkle of her eyes. If she'd lain wakeful after what they'd learned, it didn't show.

"Good morning. Did you sleep well?"

He didn't want to tell her he'd been unable to oust the private investigator's call from his mind long enough to get a good night's sleep.

"Okay." He crossed to the desk and leaned one hip against it. "What are you working on?"

"Sorting through the bills." She wrinkled her nose. "I have to confess, it's not my favorite chore, but it has to be done."

"Speaking of chores, I've decided to go to Charleston today. I want to push the private investigator for results." The need to take action pricked at his nerves, demanding movement.

Miranda's face clouded at his words. "You can't do that."

"Why not?" Everything in him steeled at her opposition. "I can't just sit around and wait, Miranda. I'd think you'd be as eager as I am to get this thing cleared up."

"Of course I am." Her voice was tart. "But you're forgetting what day this is."

His gaze sought the large calendar posted on the wall behind the desk. Had he missed a holiday?

"Sammy's off from school today, and we promised to take him to Angel Isle, remember?"

The realization that he'd let something so important to Sammy slip hit a sore spot. It might be more difficult than he'd expected to avoid repeating his father's mistakes.

He pushed himself erect. "I didn't remember we'd planned that trip for today, that's true. That doesn't mean I don't care."

"I didn't mean to imply—" She stopped, shook her head. "Sorry. Just because I keep Sammy's calendar in my head doesn't mean that you have to. I'm used to juggling what everyone's doing."

If they married, they'd have to find a way to get past this kind of misunderstanding. Again he wondered if she'd find the benefits of marriage worth the cost.

He shook off the thought. One thing at a time. He had to get this business of the photo resolved.

"Look, can't we postpone the trip to another day?" He gestured toward the window. "Cloudy as it is, it's not a nice day for an outing, anyway."

"Sammy's not going to think a few clouds are a good enough excuse not to take the boat out. If you want to change the plans, you'd better talk to him."

She picked up an envelope and slit it open. Apparently she was ready to get on with her work, no matter what her attitude was.

"I thought maybe you'd tell him for me." He leaned forward persuasively. "You could explain I had to go in to work."

"Not a chance." She glanced at him, and he saw the amusement in her eyes. "Nice try, but I'm not going to be the bearer of bad news for you. I've already told you that. You'll have to do it yourself."

Apparently Miranda had been giving some thought to how this whole parenting thing worked out between them, too.

"So Daddy doesn't just get to be the giver of gifts and leave the unpopular stuff to Mommy."

"That's right. Breaking bad news is equal opportunity. If you want—" She stopped abruptly.

The smile slid from his face. Miranda was staring at the paper she'd pulled out of an envelope, and her face had grown pale under the tan.

"Miranda? What is it?" He went quickly around the desk to put his hand on her shoulder. "Bad news?"

"I don't know." She looked at him, her expression apprehensive. "I'm not sure what this means."

"What is it?" He leaned over, focusing on the paper in her hand. A phone bill, he realized. "Bell South make a costly mistake?"

"It's last month's itemized long-distance calls." She pointed to a line. "That's a call he made—the man who took the picture of Sammy. I recognize the area code." She looked at him, eyes wide. "He called someone in Baltimore."

"What?" He snatched the page from her, running his gaze along the column to find the call, anticipation mounting. This was an unexpected stroke of luck. Maybe he wouldn't have to wait for the investigator to pry loose the information. The telephone number would be a shortcut.

He stared, his mind unwillingly processing the information in front of him.

"Tyler?" Miranda pushed her chair back to stand very close to him, her hair brushing his shoulder as she leaned over to look at the bill. "Why are you looking that way?"

"Because I know the number." Certainty hardened in him. "It happens to be the private number of a man I'd have said I could trust with almost anything. My assistant, Henry Carmichael."

"Your assistant? I don't understand." She leaned against his arm as she studied the bill. "How can that be? Are you sure?"

"I'm sure, all right." Already the shock was passing, to be replaced with anger that ate its way along his veins. "Good old Henry has sold me out."

"You can't know that." Miranda's response was swift. "There might be a dozen explanations."

"Name one." He shot the words at her, annoyed at her naiveté.

"Well, suppose he found out about Sammy somehow and just thought you should know. He could have been trying to do a good thing."

"If he thought that, he'd have told me."

"But—"

"Forget it, Miranda. I know exactly what happened. I could practically write the script. Henry's doing something he doesn't want me to find out about, and he looked for something that would distract me." Bitterness edged his words. If there was anyone he thought he could rely on, it was Henry. He'd been wrong.

"Why would he do that? I don't understand."

No, she wouldn't. The people she knew didn't do things like that.

"At a guess, it's something to do with this deal we've been working on. There's a lot of money at stake. Possibly someone from a rival firm made Henry an offer too good to pass up. It might be worth a lot to be sure I was otherwise occupied at the crucial time.''

Conviction formed even as he said the words. That had to be it.

''How can you be so sure?'' Miranda obviously thought he was jumping to conclusions.

''The timing's too perfect. They'd think with me out of the way and only Josh left in the office from the family, they'd have clear sailing. Well, they're going to find they're wrong.'' Fury hardened to implacable determination.

''What are you going to do?'' Apprehension filled her voice. Because she was worried about him? He wasn't sure.

''I'm going to Baltimore.'' He spun, the telltale bill clutched in his hand. ''Henry's going to regret this to his dying day, I can promise you that.''

''Tyler, please listen for a moment.''

''Maybe my father had a point, after all. Don't rely on anyone else, that's what he always said. They'll let you down every time.'' He stalked to the doorway. ''Well, this time they're not going to get away with it.''

She took a step toward him. ''Please, don't go into this angry. Don't do something you'll regret later.''

He shook his head, making an effort to focus on Miranda's face. ''This is business.''

Funny. That was the phrase he'd heard all his life, always said meaning that this was more important than anything else.

''Maybe you should let Josh handle it.''

"No."

He saw the hurt in her eyes at his abrupt tone. He was sorry for it, but he couldn't do anything else. This was something he had to take care of himself.

Miranda didn't understand that. The truth was, she probably never would.

Miranda sank into her chair, staring at the closed door. Tyler was leaving. From the moment she'd shown him that bill, his path was as irreversible as a tidal wave. He hadn't given a thought to Sammy or to her once his decision was made.

*Please, Lord.* The prayer came automatically, then she realized she didn't know what to pray for.

*Please, Father, be with Tyler. He's angry, but he's hurting, too. Someone he trusted has betrayed him, and he's not even going to admit how painful it is.*

Tyler's face formed in her mind, hard and implacable. He looked like the man he'd been when he arrived on the island. She hadn't realized how much he'd changed in the past weeks until that moment.

*Don't let him turn back into that person, Lord. How can he be the father Sammy needs if all he thinks of is business?*

She sat for a long time, her head bent to her folded hands, trying to see her path. Finally she stood.

She probably couldn't change his decision to go to Baltimore and handle the situation himself. Maybe he did have to. But perhaps she *could* help him see that revenge wasn't the answer. For his sake, she had to try.

She walked up the steps slowly, running her hand

along the rail that had been worn smooth by generations of hands. Where were the words that would
reach him?

Tyler had made so much progress with Sammy.
She couldn't let that slip away in his obsession with
punishing the man he'd trusted. At the very least, he
should talk with Sammy. If he explained why he had
to go away, Sammy would understand. He could have
confidence that his father would be back.

*If* he'd be back. The thought chilled her. She'd
been making assumptions about his time here, about
what his relationship with Sammy would be.

Maybe she'd been making assumptions about his
relationship with her. Hadn't those kisses meant anything? Didn't they mean she was a part of his life, to
be included in the decisions he made?

Maybe not. She forced herself to beat down the
whimpering little voice that wanted to cry about her
needs, her longings. She couldn't do anything about
that. She had to try to do something about Tyler's
role as Sammy's father.

The door to his room stood ajar, and when she
knocked on it, it swung open. Tyler turned, and she
realized he was simultaneously talking on the phone
and packing a bag.

His frown lightened as he motioned her in.

"Look, everything you say is true." He spoke into
the phone. "I'm sorry I didn't pay attention to your
concerns earlier."

He was talking to his brother, obviously. Well, if
Tyler was able to admit to Josh that he hadn't been
perfect, that was an encouraging sign.

She took the shirt he'd been trying to fold one-handed and folded it neatly, then put it into the open case on the bed. She looked at him, raising her eyebrows in a question.

He nodded and pointed to a heap of clothing at the foot of the bed. She began packing it, a small measure of relief filtering through her concern. At least he wasn't packing everything. He must intend to come back.

"No, I don't want you to do that."

For a moment she thought he meant her, and her hands stilled. Then she realized he was talking to Josh.

"Look, I know you mean well, but don't do anything until I get there. I'll call you the minute I reach the city. In the meantime, just keep an eye on him." His voice hardened to implacability. "I don't want Henry to suspect a thing."

He snapped the phone shut and paced to the table, where he began sorting through papers. "Thanks, Miranda." He sounded a thousand miles away already. "I want to get on the road to the airport as quickly as possible."

Could she say anything that would deflect his obvious desire for revenge against the person who'd wronged him? "It sounded as if your brother wanted to handle this."

"He wanted to. He's not going to." His tone told her that any discussion of that subject would be useless.

She switched gears. "Before you go, you need to explain to Sammy why you're leaving."

He slanted a look at her, his expression harassed. "I'm kind of in a hurry here, Miranda. Can't you explain it to him?"

"No, I can't." She had to make Tyler understand. "This isn't just a matter of postponing the trip we planned to take today. The fact that you're leaving will upset him. You have to be the one to reassure him."

The stern lines of his face softened, and she knew she'd reached him.

"Okay. You're right. I don't want my son getting the message from someone else that I've left."

He was comparing himself with his father again, she supposed. Maybe that was a good thing, if it meant he was determined not to make the same mistakes.

"Thank you, Tyler. When you're talking to him I hope you won't—"

He lifted his eyebrows "Won't what?"

This was difficult. "I think it's better if he doesn't feel that you're out for revenge against your assistant, no matter what he's done to you."

"A matter of values?" His voice was soft, and she couldn't tell whether he was angry or not.

"He's been taught that seeking revenge is wrong," she said firmly. "I don't want him getting mixed messages about that."

Their gazes clashed for a moment. Then he nodded. "All right. I won't promise to change how I deal with Henry, but I certainly won't discuss it with Sammy. Still, he's going to have to understand that sometimes business has to take priority. That doesn't mean I love him any less.''

That was probably the best she was going to get from him on that subject.

"I think Sammy will understand that." She put the last shirt in the suitcase. "Do you want anything else packed?" She gestured toward the closet.

"No." He stepped away from the desk, putting out his hand toward her. "Stay a minute, Miranda. There's something else I want to talk with you about.''

To her surprise he looked uncertain. That wasn't an expression she was used to seeing on Tyler's face, and it sent a shiver of apprehension through her.

"Is anything wrong?''

"Not exactly. I've just been giving a lot of thought to what our lives are going to be like in the future— Sammy's, yours, mine. I'm sure you've been doing the same thing.''

She nodded. Tyler didn't need to know she had been cherishing some totally unreasonable hopes about that life.

"We'll have to work out some kind of schedule so that he sees you often.''

"You said once that he wasn't a package to be shipped back and forth. I didn't understand what you meant then, but I do now.''

She wasn't sure where he was headed. "If Sammy's going to spend time with you in Baltimore, I guess he'll have to get used to traveling. That's the only option.''

"It's not the best one.'' He crossed the few feet

between them and took both of her hands in his. "I've given this a lot of thought. I think I know what's best for Sammy. He needs to have his parents together. We need to be a real family."

Her knees went suddenly weak. "Wh—what do you mean?" He couldn't mean what she thought he did.

"I want you to marry me, Miranda." His grasp tightened, sending a thousand unspoken messages along her skin. "Will you marry me again?"

Her heart swelled until she thought it would burst out of her chest and float to the ceiling. Tyler loved her. After all that had happened, after all this time, Tyler loved her. They were going to have the marriage she'd always dreamed about.

Apparently taking her stunned silence for doubt, he rubbed his fingers over her knuckles. "I wanted to bring this up now so you can think it over while I'm away."

Think it over? Some caution sounded through the singing in her soul.

"Look, I know this won't be the romantic fairy tale we once thought we'd have, but we're not those young kids anymore, are we?"

It took a moment to process his words. I am, she wanted to cry, but she couldn't. She could only look at him, feeling the hope drain out of her.

"You must see that marriage is the sensible solution. It's not as though either of us is involved with anyone else. We both want to put Sammy first, and getting married is the best way to do that, don't you agree?"

A business deal. Obviously that was all this was to him. He didn't imagine marriage could mean anything else to her.

He was waiting for her answer. He'd said he wanted to give her time to consider, but he obviously didn't think it was necessary. He expected her to agree with him.

The longing to do just that overwhelmed her. She wanted—oh, how much she wanted—to say yes. To be Tyler's wife again, the way she longed to be.

It wasn't right. She knew that deep in her soul. God wanted more for His dearly loved children than that. Whether Tyler knew it or not, they both deserved better from marriage.

"Miranda?" He was smiling, confident.

"I'm sorry, Tyler." How much it cost to pull her hands away from his, knowing she might never feel his touch again. "I don't think that would work."

His expression was stunned, disbelieving. "Not work? Why wouldn't it work? You can't deny it would be best for Sammy."

She took a deep breath, willing herself not to cry in front of him. "I don't agree with you. Sammy won't benefit from seeing his parents in a marriage that isn't real."

Anger flared in his eyes and declared itself in the taut lines of his face. "I'm offering you a marriage that's real in every way I can make it. I'm not suggesting we pretend anything."

"You're asking that we pretend the most important thing of all." Couldn't he see that? Her head throbbed. "Tyler, you're asking me to take vows before God to love and cherish—vows that you don't mean. I can't do that.''

''Grow up, Miranda. Half the marriages that are based on romantic love end up in the divorce court. We're the living proof of that, aren't we?'' He gripped her hands tighter, as if he could pressure the answer he wanted from her. ''We'd have caring and respect between us. And the attraction is still there. We both know that. Isn't that enough?''

Again she felt the insidious temptation to say yes— to have as much of Tyler as he was willing to offer. But she couldn't.

''No.'' Her voice trembled on the verge of tears, and she held them back with a fierce effort. ''I'm sorry, Tyler. It's not enough.''

She could almost imagine she saw something die in his eyes.

''Fine.'' He flung her hands away from him, then snatched his bag. ''If that's what you want, that's how it will be.''

He was walking away. She wanted to stop him, whatever the cost. She couldn't. She could only watch him disappear out the door.

She sank onto the edge of the bed, letting the hot, salty tears spill once he wasn't there to see. She'd had everything she wanted there in her hands, and she'd let it go.

No. She wiped the tears away with an impatient hand, but they persisted. Tyler hadn't offered what she really wanted and needed. He hadn't proposed a marriage based on love and blessed by God.

Ironic that, once she'd finally seen she could cope

with his world, he'd made her the one offer she couldn't accept. If God's love made her fit for any society, it also made her deserving of a real love.

Tyler couldn't see she offered what he needed so desperately to fill that aching void inside him left by his loveless childhood. He needed her love, but he couldn't admit it. He was trying to cheat. He wanted to fake a solution that didn't require risking his heart.

She couldn't help him do that. Even if it meant a lifetime of grieving for what they might have had, she couldn't.

She'd have to trust that God could see a way out of this, because she couldn't.

# *Chapter Fifteen*

Could this day get any worse? Tyler sat in the corporate jet that was supposed to rush him anywhere he needed to be. He stared at sullen clouds and rain spattering against the window.

Sat was the operative word here. Even the best transport money could buy didn't argue with the weather.

First this day had brought the stunning news about Henry. Then had come the utter fiasco with Miranda. Then a series of storms had come up seemingly from nowhere, grounding flights and throwing his plans into disarray.

He picked up the phone. He'd better let Josh know what was happening. He didn't want his brother getting nervous and blowing everything.

"I thought you'd be on your way by now." Josh sounded as jittery as he'd feared.

"That's because you haven't checked the weather

in Savannah. I can't go anywhere until they let us take off. What's happening there?''

"Henry's been closeted in his office all day, making calls. Do you want me to try and find out who he's calling?''

"I don't want you to do anything!''

His brother's silence told him that his reaction had come out a lot more explosively than he'd intended.

"Sorry.'' It wasn't fair to take his frustrations out on the one person who was trying to help him. "I didn't mean to blow up at you.''

"Is something wrong? Besides the obvious, I mean.'' Josh sounded as if he really wanted to know.

Tyler realized in a moment of surprise that he wanted to confide in his brother. He had to talk to someone, and there wasn't anyone else. He looked at that fact bleakly. It was a sad comment on his life.

"Things aren't going well here right now, and the timing of this situation didn't help any.''

"Things aren't going well with Sammy or with Miranda?''

Josh's perception startled him.

"How did you get so smart about relationships all of a sudden?''

"Lots of observation,'' Josh said. He chuckled. "Not personal experience, I assure you.''

"I guess not.'' Maybe that was the point of his brother's habit of never appearing with the same woman twice. Josh was as wary of relationships as Tyler was. "Our family life didn't prepare us for anything most people would call normal, did it?''

"Hardly.'' Josh hesitated a moment, and Tyler listened to the spatter of the rain and the static on the phone. "You know, our family to the contrary, plenty of people manage to create real marriages for themselves. Maybe even a Winchester could do that."

"Maybe." There didn't seem much else to say. "Hold the fort. I'll be there as soon as I can."

He put the phone away, but Josh's words seemed to hang in the air. Some people manage to create real marriages for themselves.

Real? The word lodged in his mind, resisting his effort to ignore it.

Real wasn't what he'd offered Miranda. She'd been wise enough to see that.

If he'd really proposed, if he'd told her he didn't know if he had it in him to love someone but he wanted to try, what would she have said then?

*You'll never know, because you don't have guts enough to risk it.*

The thought came out of nowhere, shaking him. Was that it? Was he really too afraid?

He took a hard look at the possibilities. The alternative seemed to be living his father's life over again, relying on no one, substituting business success for personal success, having no decent relationships with any of the people he loved.

Love. The word terrified him, and that was the truth of it. He'd been determined to love no one. Then Sammy came along.

He hadn't had a choice about being Sammy's father. Loving him had been inevitable and irrevocable. Miranda was another story.

He'd played it safe. Disgust at himself welled up

suddenly. He'd made a halfhearted offer of a half-baked marriage, and he'd expected Miranda to jump at the chance. Was it any wonder she'd been revolted? He hadn't even taken the time to do it right, trying to sandwich in asking her to be his wife between business calls and rushing off to Baltimore.

He saw what he had to do, and it scared him. If he wanted to make things work with Miranda and Sammy, he had to be honest with them. He had to show them that he would put them first. There was a way to do that, if he could.

For a long moment he stared at the phone in his hand. Then he punched in his brother's number.

"Josh Winchester speaking."

"I want you to handle this situation with Henry," Tyler said, not bothering with the pleasantries.

"What?" Josh's voice sounded far away, as if he'd removed the phone from his ear to stare at it, incredulous. "Are you sure about that?"

"I'm sure." Suddenly he was smiling. "You're not any less prepared to take over than I was when Dad died. You can do it."

"But what if Warren doesn't want to go through with the deal? You know the competition has probably lowballed us, based on whatever info Henry sold them."

He could see only one way to handle this, and Josh could do it as well as he could.

"Go in there prepared to sell them all over again. The bottom line is, we can give them the best product at the best price, regardless of what Henry's done." He hoped Josh could hear the conviction in his voice.

"You can do this. And when the meeting's over, either way, you can have the pleasure of firing Henry, with my compliments."

"If you say so."

Through the doubt, Tyler heard a new sense of responsibility in his brother's voice. For some reason it made him think of Miranda's father talking about how he'd let his brother down by not forgiving him for his mistakes and trusting him again.

"I say so," he said firmly.

"What are you going to be doing while I'm playing chief?"

"Trying to put my family back together again, if I can."

"You can." Josh sounded confident. "Good luck."

If. He hung up, trying not to think how iffy this really was. Whatever the chance, he was doing the right thing.

He ran through the drizzle to the rental car. Josh deserved the chance to see what he could do. And Tyler—well, deserve it or not, he wanted a chance to convince Miranda that they could build a life together.

Eager to hear her voice, he called the inn as he drove toward the island. It was her father, not Miranda, who answered.

"Thought you were on your way north." Clayton sounded wary.

"I made a mistake," he said. "I'm on my way back now. Where is Miranda?"

"Well, Sammy was right disappointed about not

going to Angel Isle today, so Miranda decided to take him.''

''In this weather?'' Fear gripped him.

Clayton must have heard it. ''Now, there's no cause to be upset. They left in plenty of time to be there before these storms come up. Miranda will have them snug in the cottage until the weather clears, count on it.''

''You're sure they'd have gotten there?''

''Certain sure. You just come on back home. These storms will blow off before you know it.''

Relieved, he put the phone down and put both hands on the wheel. Fierce wind buffeted the car, and the drainage ditches on either side of the road showed an alarming tendency to spill over onto the surface. Clayton said the storms would blow over soon, and he certainly knew the weather on the islands as well as anyone. They'd be okay.

That assurance was growing thin by the time he battled his way across the bridge. Each line of thunderstorms was succeeded by another, equally bad. Impelled by fear for Miranda and Sammy that grew with each rumble of thunder and crack of lightning, he pulled to a stop at the dock in front of Adam's boat yard. He spotted Adam tying up a small motorboat.

He stepped into a downpour that soaked him through in seconds and ran toward the dock. The fear that rode him quadrupled. He had to get to them. He couldn't explain it logically, but he knew in his bones he had to get to them.

''Now we'll be warm in no time at all.'' Shivering, Miranda touched a match to the paper she'd crumpled under the kindling in the fireplace. She smiled at Sammy, hoping she sounded calm and confident.

A blast of wind rattled the windows in spite of the storm shutters they'd closed, and apprehension widened Sammy's eyes. "D'you think it's going to last a long time, Momma?"

"Oh, I don't think so." Flames licked around the pine knots, catching quickly. She held out her hands to the welcome warmth. "Even if it does, we're okay, aren't we? We've got a fire to keep us warm, a roof to keep us dry, and we can probably find something to eat in the kitchen if we need it. It's an adventure."

He grinned at her with his father's smile, shattering her heart yet again. "I'll bet none of the cousins got stuck here in such a bad storm."

"You can tell them all about it, can't you?" She put her arm around his shoulder.

He leaned against her, relaxing. "I hope the storm lasts till suppertime, so we can cook hot dogs over the fire. And marshmallows."

Apparently her words had calmed his fears. Now if only she could calm her own, she'd be all right.

Where was Tyler? She suppressed a shiver. He'd set off to fly to Baltimore. Would the plane be safely above the storms by now? Or was he stuck on the ground in Savannah, raging against the freak weather that kept him from being where he wanted to be?

Her heart ached so strongly she rubbed her hand against her chest, as if that would ease the burden. Sammy had taken the news that his father had to go away with disappointment but no doubts that he would be back. He'd probably talk Tyler into another trip to Angel Isle, based on the argument that this trip was supposed to involve all three of them.

All three of them. The image made her heartache worse. If she'd said yes to Tyler, they'd have looked forward to a lifetime of all three of them.

No, not a lifetime. Sammy would grow up, go off to college, have a life of his own. That was the way it should be. What would she and Tyler have done then, tied in a marriage that wasn't real?

She'd dreamed, often enough, of growing old with Tyler, but not that way. Not living as two separate individuals trapped in the same house, existing politely in a vacuum.

As God's dearly beloved children…

God had something better in mind for those He loved. She had to believe that.

Sammy stirred. ''You think we could make some popcorn in the fireplace?''

''Hungry already?'' she teased, ruffling his hair. ''Sure, I guess so. You go pick out a game you'd like to play, and I'll get the popcorn and popper out.''

He was up in an instant. Another boom of thunder sounded, very close, and she saw the flicker of fear in his eyes, quickly masked.

''I'll get Monopoly, okay? Then it'll be okay if the storm lasts a long time.''

She gave him a reassuring smile, and he ran through the kitchen toward the game room they'd added years ago to the cottage. She followed, hoping the popcorn jars in the kitchen were full. Sammy would be disappointed if his adventure didn't include popcorn, and probably hot dogs, as well. Since the storm didn't show any signs of letting up, he'd probably get his wish.

She pushed through the kitchen door, looking through the opposite door to the game room. They'd never bothered to put storm shutters on those windows, since the wind didn't come from that direction. That seemed small comfort in a storm like this. Sheets of rain drove against the exposed panes, and the wind whipped the palmettos and live oaks into a frenzy of ripping leaves and torn Spanish moss.

She paused, hand reaching for the popcorn jar on the shelf above the stove. Sammy was safe enough in the walk-in closet where the games were stored, but the turmoil outside the windows still made her uneasy.

"Sammy, grab the game and hurry in here," she called. "Let's get back to the fireplace where it's warm."

"Okay, Momma, I'm coming."

She heard the game hit the floor, then Sammy muttering something about dropping it. Lightning cracked again, illuminating the wild scene outside the windows in an eerie light. The clap of thunder followed so closely they were almost simultaneous. Apprehension skittered along her skin, and she put the jar down.

"Come on, sugar. I'll get it." She stepped into the game room, heading for the closet.

Lightning cracked again, so close the acrid scent filled the air. Another crack burst on her ears, even louder than the thunder. The hundred-year-old live oak outside the windows shuddered. Before she could move, it fell. The room collapsed around her in a kaleidoscope of shattering walls and flying debris.

She was on the floor, a chair lying across her legs. She struggled to her feet. Sammy. She had to get to her son.

"Sammy, where are you?" She looked around, completely disoriented. The room was a shambles of broken siding and shattered glass. "Sammy!"

"I'm okay, Momma." His voice was reassuringly near. "But I can't get up."

"Hold on, sugar. I'm coming." She battled a few steps, shoving debris aside. A blast of wind drove a sheet of rain into her face, and the cold shock cleared her head.

*Please, Lord.* "Sammy, say something!"

"I'm here. In the closet."

*Thank You, Lord.*

She stumbled across the room, dashing the water from her eyes so she could see. The doorframe was still there, the walls surrounding it still upright. She clambered over a fallen beam and made it through the door.

"I'm okay, Momma, but I can't get out." Sammy's anxious face peered at her through a tangle of boards. The shelves had come down, boxing him into a small den behind them.

"I'll get you out. Don't you worry." She forced her voice to remain steady while panic ripped along her nerves. She grabbed the nearest board, yanking it free.

*Please, God, please, God, give me the strength to get him out.*

"I'll help," Sammy said, but when he pushed on a board, the wall above him swayed ominously.

"Don't, honey, don't. We have to take them away carefully." She fought for calm. "Like playing jack-straws. We don't want them to topple over."

Cautiously she lifted out one board, then another. She could reach through the hole and touch him, and she stroked his cheek.

"Just one more, then you can wiggle out."

She grasped the heavy beam. It wouldn't move. She braced her feet against a pile of rubble and pulled again. It remained stubbornly immovable. Another crack of lightning lit the room, showing her Sammy's scared face.

She had to get him out. If another piece of the roof fell, they could both be buried. She tugged again, hands tearing against the rough wood, muscles screaming.

*Help me, Lord, help me. I'm not strong enough. Help me!*

"Miranda! Sammy!"

She recognized his voice even while her logical mind told her there was no way on earth Tyler could be there. He climbed into the closet beside her, running his hands down her arms, trying to pull her away from the beam.

"No, I have to—"

"I'll get it, love." His voice was deep, reassuring. "Just move back a little."

She couldn't. He had to unclasp her hands, lift her

away. She felt his strength as he maneuvered past her, wedging himself into the space she'd occupied.

"How are you doing, son?"

He was so calm he might have been asking how Sammy's day at school had been, but she had glimpsed the anguish in his eyes.

"I'm okay, Daddy." Sammy's voice trembled a little. "I'm glad you're here."

"Me, too, son." Tyler gave an experimental tug at the beam, then nodded to Miranda. "It's wedged too tightly to pull out," he said softly. "I'll have to push it up. As soon as I clear enough space, you pull him out."

She nodded, not sure she trusted her voice to speak. Tyler stooped and wedged his back under the beam, bracing his hands against the wall. With another glance at her, he began to push.

The beam remained stubbornly immobile. Lightning cracked again, seeming to give Tyler more strength. He pushed harder, face taut, muscles tight. The beam creaked, groaned, then began to inch upward.

The hole through which she'd touched Sammy's face widened a little, then a little more. She reached through, her legs pressing against Tyler's. His were solid as rock, holding danger away from their son.

She got both hands around Sammy's shoulders. "Almost enough," she breathed. "Just a little more."

The veins in Tyler's temples stood out. Eyes closed, he pushed harder—surely beyond the limit of his human strength.

*Help him, Lord. Help us.*

She clutched their son, began pulling him through the space made by his father's strength.

"It's okay, sugar. Just a little more."

She had him out far enough that he could clasp her around the neck. She tugged, and he was free.

She hugged him tight. "He's all right. I've got him. You can let go now."

Tyler shook his head, sweat pouring off his face. "Get him out before I let go."

What would the whole precarious stack do when he let go? It could come down on him.

"I'll help you—"

"Out!" It was nearly a shout, and it propelled her backward out of the closet, into the rain again. She clutched Sammy close, breathing a frightened prayer.

*Protect him, Lord. Don't let me lose him now, please.*

The remaining walls seemed to shudder, and a cloud of dust erupted from the closet.

"Tyler!"

Even as she cried his name, he emerged from the smoke. His arms circled both of them. They stumbled to the shelter of the kitchen.

Safe. God be praised, they were safe.

# *Chapter Sixteen*

They weren't safe yet. Gasping from the pain in his back and shoulders, Tyler grabbed Miranda and Sammy, hustling them through the kitchen and into the large living room. Closing the door behind them instantly muted the roar of the storm, and he saw with relief that storm shutters protected the windows.

"Are you all right?" Miranda pulled free from his arms, her attention on Sammy. She took his face between her hands, then ran her fingers through his hair. "Does it hurt anywhere?"

Sammy wiggled, impatient at being held. "I'm okay, Momma. Don't fuss."

Tyler caressed his son's face as he set him on his feet. "That's what mothers do, son. Be glad of it."

"What about you?" Miranda was looking at Tyler with an expression he couldn't interpret. "Are you hurt?"

He stretched cautiously. "Nothing permanently damaged."

He saw her hands then, and caught them in his, turning the palms up to reveal the abrasions. Something winced inside him at the thought of Miranda struggling alone, without him, ripping her hands trying to free their son.

*Thank You, Lord.* The passion in his prayer caught him unaware. *Thank You.*

"It's nothing." She tried to pull her hands away, but he held them fast.

"We need to get those cleaned up." He glanced around. "Is there water somewhere?"

"Should be jugs under the kitchen sink." She shivered as thunder boomed, and he caressed her wrists lightly.

"Sounds like it's moving off."

She nodded, and he thought she drew on some reserve of strength to speak naturally. "Even if it gets worse again, this part of the original building will be safe. It's gone through a couple of hurricanes without falling."

He turned her toward the sofa. "You relax. I'll get the water."

He opened the door to the kitchen cautiously, but the room seemed secure. The room beyond, the addition Miranda said they'd built when her father was a teenager, had taken the brunt of the damage. He found a water jug and hurried back to Miranda and Sammy.

They were snuggled close together on the sofa, and he stood for a moment, looking at them, his heart overflowing. They were safe and together. At the moment nothing else seemed significant.

"Here we go." He set the water jug on the coffee table, then dampened the dish towel he'd found on the counter.

"I can manage," Miranda protested, but he clasped her hands and began to sponge her palms gently.

"Let Daddy," Sammy said. He looked at Tyler with something that might have been awe in his eyes. "I knew you'd come."

It was what he'd said when he was trapped in the closet and Tyler had been terrified he wouldn't be able to get him out.

"I came," he said. "But how did you know?"

"'Cause I prayed." Sammy wiggled a little closer to his mother. "When I was scared, I asked God to help us. And I asked Him to send you. And He did."

"You know what?" Tyler smiled at his son. "I prayed the same thing. God must have heard both of us."

He sensed Miranda's measuring gaze on him as he cradled her hand in his to clean her cuts. She must be wondering whether he meant what he said.

She couldn't know how the past weeks had gradually opened the long-closed doors of his soul. He hadn't known it himself until he'd instinctively turned to God when he'd been afraid for them.

Whatever Miranda saw must have satisfied her, because she nodded. "All three of us," she said softly. "He heard all of us."

He held her hands, his gaze meeting hers. Probably the question he wanted to ask showed in his face. Could she see that?

She moved a little, drawing her hands away, glancing at Sammy. "Maybe—" She sounded a little breathless. "Maybe we ought to try to get through to the family. They'll be worried." She smiled suddenly. "You do have your cell phone, don't you?"

He pulled it from his pocket and handed it over, wondering what she was thinking. Did she know how much he longed for a private moment with her, so he could try to repair the damage he'd done with his clumsy proposal?

He studied her face as she spoke with her father, cherishing the curve of her cheek, the generous mouth, the love in her eyes. He hoped he heard caring in her voice when she told her father that Tyler was there, that thanks to Tyler they were safe.

Was it selfish to want more than safety? He had to find a way to let her know how much he cared—to convince her that he didn't want a fake marriage. He wanted the real thing.

Miranda tucked an afghan over Sammy, who was curled up asleep in the big easy chair. The storm had ended, but not before they'd dined on hot dogs and marshmallows. Then, suddenly exhausted, Sammy had fallen asleep in the middle of a sentence.

Tyler added another log to the fire, then leaned his elbow on the mantel. He'd lost his tie somewhere along the line, and he'd pulled on an old flannel shirt of her father's in place of the dress shirt that had been ripped and filthy. The mismatched clothing, the shadow of a beard, his tousled hair only served to make him more handsome.

He glanced at Sammy. "He's wiped out."

She sank onto the sofa. "So am I. It's just as well we decided to stay here until morning. I'd probably have run the boat aground if we tried to go back tonight."

The rain spattered gently against the windows as Tyler came to sit next to her. Her nerves jumped. With Sammy asleep, they were alone.

The hurtful words they'd spoken to each other when they parted returned to haunt her. What if he intended to repeat his proposal? How would she ever summon the strength to say no again?

He touched her wrist, and her pulse fluttered.

"How—how could you come to the island today?" Any question would do to keep him from knowing how she felt when he was near. "What happened to the deal?"

For an instant he looked blank, then he shook his head, smiling. "Hard as it is to believe, I'd actually forgotten all about it. I put Josh in charge." His gaze lingered on her face, so warm he might as well have been touching her skin. "I had other things on my mind."

She swallowed. She had to remember that nothing had really changed. He still wanted a sham of a marriage that she couldn't accept.

"Maybe you ought to call him and find out what happened." Anything to put off the moment when he'd ask her again, when she'd have to try to find the courage to refuse again.

She felt his gaze on her face and stubbornly refused to look at him. Finally he drew away a few inches and picked up the phone.

While he talked, she studied her hands, folded in her lap, and tried not to let herself think about what it would be like to be Tyler's wife again.

"Good job, Josh. I knew you could do it."

The warmth in his voice pleased her. Apparently he and his brother had found some common ground at last.

"No, I don't want to prosecute. Just let him leave. He can't hurt us any longer."

He exchanged a few more words, then hung up. She looked at him questioningly. "It went all right?"

"Very much so. Josh handled everything perfectly." He gave her a rueful smile. "Maybe better than I would have. Seems I've been underestimating my little brother."

"You trusted him today."

His hand closed over hers, setting her pulse thudding. "Thanks to you."

"Me?"

"Your family," he amended. "If I hadn't been here, seen how all of you rely on each other, I might never have taken the risk." His gaze, very serious, rested on her. "I remembered something your father said about how he'd never trusted his brother again after that business when the dolphin was lost, that maybe his distrust kept his brother from being the man he should have been. I didn't want to wake up and feel that about Josh twenty years from now."

"I'm glad," she said, wondering if he could hear the joy she felt that he'd made peace with his brother. "And I'm glad you decided not to prosecute Henry."

He squeezed her hand. "'You meant it for evil, but

God meant it for good.' You quoted that verse to me, remember? Henry sent that photograph for his own ends, but it brought me Sammy. I couldn't punish him for that."

*Thank you, Lord.* The prayer was whispered in her heart. Tyler was becoming the man God intended him to be. Whatever happened between them, he'd be a better father for that.

"You know, you didn't ask the right question."

She looked at him, startled. "What right question?"

"You asked how I could come back. You didn't ask why I came back."

She was suddenly breathless, and her heart seemed to be beating in her throat. She managed a whisper. "Why did you?"

He lifted her hand gently to his lips. "Because I did it all wrong when I asked you to marry me." His voice was husky, and she felt his breath against her fingers as he spoke. "I tried to cheat. I tried to get what I wanted without risking my heart."

She couldn't speak to save herself, but he didn't seem to expect it.

"I was kidding myself, you know that, don't you? You already had my heart right here." He turned her hand over, dropped the lightest of kisses in her bruised palm. "I love you, Miranda, with all my heart. Please marry me again. Let us have a real marriage—the one that God intended for us."

Joy bubbled inside her until she thought it would lift her right into the air. In spite of the darkness outside, she could almost hear a bird singing, giving wings to her heart.

She reached to touch his dear face. "Don't you know I've never stopped loving you?" She traced the outline of his lips with her fingertip. "Yes, Tyler. I've never stopped being your wife."

She saw the sheen of tears in his eyes through a haze of joy. His lips claimed hers, and she thought her heart would burst with loving him.

What was meant to be from the beginning was coming true. Their love had been broken. Now it was mended, and it would be all the stronger.

A clatter on the porch woke Miranda. For an instant she thought the house was coming down around them. Then she sat up and smiled at Tyler, waking on the sofa.

"Time to get up. Sounds as if the family has arrived."

Sammy had already jumped up and run to the door. In a moment the room was filled with Caldwells, all of them talking at once. All exclaiming, hugging, kissing. Tyler looked embarrassed at all the emotion, but he was smiling.

"Not much left but matchsticks out there," her father said, coming in from the kitchen. "Still, we may as well start clearing up. Jeff and his boys just pulled in, and Adam's brought equipment from the boatyard."

Tyler stretched. "I'll come and help you."

"No need, son." Her father clapped his shoulder. "You've done more than your share already. Get some breakfast and coffee in you first. I reckon Sallie brought some clothes for y'all, too.''

"That I did.'' Sallie handed him a bag, then enveloped him in a hug. "God bless you, Tyler. Thank you.''

He drew back, as if not sure how to react, but Miranda saw pleasure in his eyes. "Just thank God," he said. "That's enough.''

Miranda disengaged herself from Chloe's hug, wondering whether the happiness in their faces had already given away the announcement they'd need to make once they'd told Sammy. Her heart clenched. Would he be as happy as she hoped?

From outside, one of the twins yelled at the kids to stay away from the wreckage. "Let's go upstairs and change.'' She took Tyler's arm. "Maybe by that time they'll have stopped making so much noise.''

Tyler grinned as he followed her. "I don't think it'll get any better.''

She showed him into one of the bedrooms, then started for the other side of the hall to change. Realizing she hadn't taken her clothes from the bag, she turned back.

"Tyler, I forgot '' She stopped. He'd taken his shirt off, revealing the dark bruise the beam had left clear across his back.

She went to him, touching him with a murmur of distress. When he'd been tending her hands, he must have been in pain. "Why didn't you tell me you were hurting? We ought to get you to a doctor.''

He took her hands in his. "I don't need a doctor. But I could use a kiss.''

She smiled at him, still troubled. "You can always have that."

He'd barely touched her lips when the door creaked. Which of her kin had decided to interrupt them now?

Their son stood in the doorway. She wasn't sure what to say, and she suspected Tyler didn't have a clue, either.

Sammy solved it for them. "Are you going to get married again?"

"We want to." Tyler spoke before Miranda could. "Would that be okay with you?"

Sammy surveyed them solemnly, then nodded. Suddenly he rushed across the room and threw himself at them. That three-way hug was probably the best thing she had ever felt in her life.

Too soon, Sammy wiggled free. Uncertainty clouded his eyes. "Will we have to live up north?"

"I've been thinking about that." Tyler glanced at her, as if measuring her approval. "We've got some ideas for expanding our companies in the southeast, so I thought maybe we could live in Charleston. That way we could have a house on the island, too, and come over as much as we wanted to."

She could hardly believe what she heard. Tyler must have been thinking about this half the night, and she knew what it cost him to make this change in his life.

"Cool," Sammy pronounced, and then darted from the room, shouting. "Hey, Gran. Guess what?"

"Somehow I don't think we'll have to tell anyone else." Tyler put his arm around Miranda again.

She searched his face. "Do you really want to do this? Because I'd live anywhere with you." She wasn't afraid any more.

"I know you would, but this is what I want. Developing something new will be a challenge for me, and Josh can be in charge in Baltimore without me looking over his shoulder all the time. Now, about that kiss—"

This time the interruption came in the form of a shout from outside. A ripple of fear told her she hadn't totally recovered from yesterday's terror. "We'd best see what's happening."

Tyler clasped her hand in his as they went quickly down the stairs and out the door. Everyone seemed to be gathered around the wreckage next to the kitchen.

Miranda hurried to Gran. "What is it? What's Daddy doing?"

Her father squatted in the midst of the fallen wall next to the kitchen, carefully unearthing something.

"It was in between the uprights where they put the addition on that summer." Gran looked as if she were talking in a dream. "Your daddy just spotted the tip of it."

"What, Gran?" She clutched her grandmother's arm, frightened at the strained look on her face. "What did he find?"

"The dolphin," someone said in a whisper. "It must be the dolphin."

Her father looked up, seeming to search until he found the face he wanted. "Jeff," he called to his brother. "Come help me get it out."

Uncle Jeff clambered over the wreckage, his face taut.

Miranda clung to Tyler with one hand, to Gran with the other. They'd mourned the loss of the dolphin for so long. If they found it now, only to discover it broken to bits as a result of the storm—

Daddy and Uncle Jeff stood up. In their upraised hands the Caldwell dolphin soared upward, as if it leaped toward the sky.

Tears spilled onto her cheeks. "We found it." She turned into Tyler's arms. "After all this time, we found it."

"That poor girl must have hidden it in the wall that night and never had a chance to tell anyone." Gran's eyes were bright with tears. "It's lain there all these years, waiting to be found in God's own time."

Miranda leaned her forehead against Tyler's chest. "Suppose you think we're foolish, to get so excited over an old carving."

He tipped her face up. "Nothing foolish about it. Like your grandmother said, what was lost is found again. Nobody knows that better than we do."

She smiled through her tears, understanding. They'd lost each other, too, but finally, in God's own time, they'd found each other again, for keeps.

# *Epilogue*

Tyler stood at the chancel of St. Andrew's Church, waiting for his bride. He took a steadying breath and glanced across the few feet that separated him from Miranda's cousin Adam.

It had been Gran's idea that this be a double wedding—Adam and Tory, Tyler and Miranda. He hadn't been sure at first about sharing this day, but he'd come to see that this was about more than their wedding. It was about family, joined together and extending into the past and into the future.

Josh, perfectly at ease in his best-man role, leaned close. "You're acquiring a lot of family today."

"Yes." He looked across the church, packed with those who'd come to wish them well. He'd once thought family meant only people who wanted something from him. Now he knew better.

Even his mother was there, all the way from Madrid and her new husband, looking dazed at the fact of being a grandmother. He still had to smile at the thought of the gracious way Miranda had welcomed her. She'd found again all the confidence she'd ever need.

His gaze intersected with Gran's, and she nodded solemnly, then looked past him to where the dolphin stood. He didn't need much imagination to know what she was thinking. Once again things had been restored to the way God intended them. The lost had been found.

The organ music swelled, and Sammy appeared at the head of the aisle next to Adam's daughter. Jenny carried a basket of flowers. Sammy stared intently at the rings he bore, then looked up and flashed a smile at his father as he began to walk toward him.

Tyler's heart lifted with the music. All this had begun with a picture of Sammy sliding onto his desk, interrupting the life he'd thought he wanted. He couldn't have guessed then that it would end this way, with wholeness restored and a richer future than he'd ever dreamed of.

The matrons of honor came next—Miranda's sister, Chloe, and Tory's new sister-in-law, Sarah. Then a rustle went through the church as the music rose triumphantly.

Miranda came toward him, radiant in the ivory gown that had been her grandmother's and the lace veil that had been handed down to generations of Caldwell brides. His throat was so tight he had a moment of panic, thinking he wouldn't be able to voice his vows.

Then she reached him, and he took her hand in his and knew he could do anything, be anything, as long as he had her love. Together they turned to face the minister.

Behind the pulpit, the Caldwell dolphin, back where it belonged, arched upward in prayer, its smile a reminder of God's eternal love and blessing.

\* \* \* \* \*

*Be sure to look for*
*Marta Perry's next book,*

*ALWAYS IN HER HEART,*

*coming in September 2003,*
*only from Steeple Hill Love Inspired.*

Dear Reader,

I'm so glad you decided to read this book. The love story of Miranda and Tyler brings the Caldwell Kin stories to a close. I've loved writing this series on the power of family, and I hate to see it end. So this has been a bittersweet story for me to write.

Maybe it was fitting that Miranda and Tyler's story closes out the family series, because their story is a tale of a broken family brought back to wholeness through the power of God's love. My prayer is that you've experienced that love in your own life.

Please let me know how you liked this story. You can reach me c/o Steeple Hill Books, 233 Broadway, New York, NY 10279, or visit me on the Web at www.martaperry.com.

Blessings,

*Marta Perry*

# Love Inspired

# HOME TO
# SAFE HARBOR

### BY

# KATE WELSH

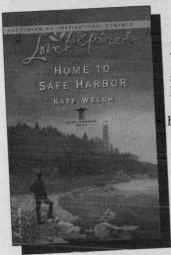

Determined to
prove herself, Reverend
Justine Clemens returned
to the town where she'd
spent her troubled youth.
Resigned to living her life
alone, she poured all her
hopes and dreams into her
new ministry. But God
clearly had other plans
for this as He brought
her head-to-head with
Chief Matthew Trent.
Would Justine finally
take a chance on love?

**Don't miss**
# HOME TO SAFE HARBOR

the final installment of
### SAFE HARBOR
*The town where everyone finds shelter from the storm!*
## On sale June 2003
*Available at your favorite retail outlet.*

Visit us at www.steeplehill.com

LIHTSH

# A LOVE TO KEEP

### BY
## CYNTHIA RUTLEDGE

Lori Loveland didn't plan on risking her heart during her six-month stint as devoted nanny to Drew McCashlin's daughters. But once she let her guard down around the handsome single dad and his beloved girls, she found herself praying that six months could last a lifetime!

**Don't miss**
## A LOVE TO KEEP
**On sale May 2003**
*Available at your favorite retail outlet.*

Visit us at www.steeplehill.com          LIALTK

# Love Inspired®

# HEAVEN KNOWS

BY

## JILLIAN HART

John Corey's soul ached for his late wife but he tried
to move forward as best he could for their beloved
little girl's sake. Like a gift from God, drifter
Alexandra Sims wandered into their lives and
turned it around. Suddenly, John began to believe
in love again, but would Alexandra's painful secret
stand in the way of true happiness?

**Don't miss**

## HEAVEN KNOWS

**On sale June 2003**

*Available at your favorite retail outlet.*

Visit us at www.steeplehill.com

LIHK

# Love Inspired®

# THE CARPENTER'S WIFE

### BY

# LENORA WORTH

No one wanted roots more than Rock Dempsey.
He finally met the woman he wanted to share his life
with in Ana Hanson. But nothing had ever come easy
for the woman he hoped to have and to hold forever.
Would it take some divine guidance from above
before she would become the carpenter's wife?

**Don't miss**
# THE CARPENTER'S WIFE
## On sale June 2003

*Available at your
favorite retail outlet.*

Visit us at www.steeplehill.com

LITCW